THE RED INN OF SAINT LYPHAR

THE RED INN
OF SAINT LYPHAR

By

ANNA T. SADLIER

ST. AIDAN PRESS, LLC
Morning View, Kentucky

The Red Inn of Saint Lyphar.

First published in 1904 by Benziger Brothers, of New York, Cincinnati, and Chicago.

Typesetting, layout and cover design copyright 2024 St. Aidan Press, LLC.

Cover art by Andrea England.

ISBN-13: 978-1-962503-05-1
ISBN-10: 1-962503-05-4

For more information, contact:
www.staidanpress.com
staidanpress@gmail.com

We have made no intentional change from the original text except to correct mistakes in spelling and punctuation.

FOR MRS. MARY HOPKINS
WHO WILL HAVE HER OWN COPY BACK NOW
WITH MANY THANKS

CONTENTS

THE RED INN
OF SAINT LYPHAR

Chapter I

Citizen Premion is Introduced

THE REVOLUTION, which in the closing years of the eighteenth century shook France from end to end, left La Vendée and the whole of Brittany for a considerable time undisturbed. So long, in fact, as the great revolt was a purely political one, it had but little effect upon that primitive population. Their nobles were, for the most part, free from the crimes and follies which had made their order odious in other parts of the kingdom. The clergy, pious and devoted, were the fathers of the people, while the people, sincerely religious, practised loyalty to the State as they practised other Christian duties.

The terrible law of 1790, declaring that each priest must take an oath acknowledging that he held his jurisdiction entirely from the State, was the torch which set La Vendée on fire. The Breton clergy to a man refused the oath, the nobles unanimously opposed it, and the peasantry, stirred to its depths, began to think seriously of stemming the torrent of the Revolution and taking the field against those who oppressed the Church. Constitutional priests were put in place of the old pastors, who wandered in the marshes or sought shelter in the thick brush of the Bocage, where their

1

people still came to them for ministration. Many of them perished on the guillotine, in the waters of the Loire, or in the quarries, and the people rose in their might to avenge them.

In the dismal year of 1793, when the nights were already growing longer and darker, a number of men were assembled, according to custom, in the parlor of the Red Inn. Their talk at first was merely of the past. Dumartin, the innkeeper, described at length the merry days of old, the fêtes in the park of the chateau, where their feudal lord, the Marquis de la Roche André, entertained the whole population of Saint Lyphar and of some of the adjoining parishes as well. The Marquis himself stood apart in conversation with some of the notables of the village, but Monsieur le Curé was everywhere, encouraging the sports, cheering on the players, and knocking at the great door of the chateau kitchen to bid those within bring out a greater abundance of good cheer. "Monsieur le Curé." There was a stern and awful silence at the name, and the furrowed cheeks of some of the older men were moistened with the tears they could not repress, while the faces of their juniors grew stern and dark. For the good pastor of Saint Lyphar had been as a father to his people, and now, after lying for many months in the prison at Nantes, because he would not take the oath of infamy required by the Government, a tragic tale had reached the village. The beloved man had perished in one of those terrible *noyades*, or drownings, by which the inhuman monster, Carrier, disposed of whole cargoes of priests and aristocrats. The Curé had died while trying to save a brother priest, who had been fastened to him with bonds, after the fashion of the revolutionary tribunals. His successor, a constitutional priest who had been sent from Paris to Saint Lyphar, had only been installed by the aid of six hundred men and four pieces of artillery, and was left without fire to light his tapers and without a solitary worshiper at the desecrated altars. For the people of Saint Lyphar preferred to steal away to hear Mass by an exiled priest who was hiding in the marshes near Saint Hilaire de Rioz.

"My friends," said a thin, dark man, speaking suddenly with curiously repressed fire and passion in his voice, "we, the people of Saint Lyphar, shall remember our beloved pastor. The example of Nicholas Tiec shall be our guide."

"Nicholas Tiec?" inquired a stranger, who had hitherto sat silent by the fire.

"Yes; Nicholas Tiec," cried a chorus of stern voices, "we shall remember."

"But what did he do, this Nicholas?" again inquired the stranger.

"He did this," said the dark man quietly. "When the Marat corps came to expel our Curé, and put his infamous successor in his place, Nicholas seized a pitchfork and opposed them single handed. The officer in command cried out to him to yield. 'First, yield me my God!' answered Nicholas."

"And then?" questioned the stranger.

"Then Nicholas fell with twenty-two wounds in him. But his spirit lives. It is ours, my friends. It is a heritage."

The stranger turned back to the fire, the sneering smile about his lips contradicted by the lowering scowl upon his brow.

"Nor was Nicholas the only one," remarked the innkeeper, "for there was Stanislas Foret."

"Aye, there was Stanislas Foret," cried the peasants, as though they were being aroused by a battle cry.

"And may I be informed who is Stanislas Foret?" asked the stranger again.

"You may, sir!" cried the dark man, turning no favorable eye upon the questioner. "He was the peasant of this parish who to our honor, sir—mark you, to our honor—permitted those cursed republicans to consume his hand with fire rather than use it to burn his Catechism, and it is his good wife, Katherine, who stood up and cried out to him: 'Well done, Stanislas, it is for the good God, and He will reward you.'"

"My friends, my very dear friends," began the stranger, beaming upon the assembly, with well feigned cordiality, "will you permit me one observation?"

"A dozen, sir, provided they be of the right sort," answered the dark man, curtly. Whereupon the stranger gave the speaker a moment's particular attention before he resumed.

"It is simply that you are far behind the times here in this lonely district of yours beside the Loire. You have not yet awakened to the evils of priestly tyranny, of superstition."

"Silence, sir," cried Dumartin, the innkeeper. "I allow none within my house to insult our clergy and our faith. They are sacred."

"Bravo, Dumartin!" cried the dark man, his exclamation being instantly echoed by the whole assembly. "And you, sir, stranger as you are in our midst, be more guarded, I warn you, in your talk, or the sacred rights of hospitality may not always protect you."

"Are you so certain, Richard Duplessis, that I am a stranger?" cried the man addressed, arising from his seat near the fire to confront the other, who had likewise arisen.

"What, you know me?" cried Duplessis in surprise; "and yet as to your being a stranger, there is no doubt about that. I was one of those who, on Monday, a fortnight since, was summoned to yonder hill first by the barking of Père Michel's dog, and next by cries for help. Dumartin here, and I, with Claude Pilon from the blacksmith's, reached the brow of the hill to see a vehicle overturned, with you underneath, and you told us, when you were able to explain, that you were from Nantes, where you had lately arrived from Paris."

The stranger nodded as if in consent, and Duplessis continued.

"Yes, you have been at the Capital, and can tell of the sittings of the States-General, the speeches of Mirabeau, the storming of the Bastile, the excitement of the populace, and a thousand things which have little to do with our once tranquil La Vendée."

"But perchance I can tell you likewise," said the other, "of summer mornings upon the Marais, where Richard Duplessis and a barefooted lad, who was called Morin-Premion, leaped the dikes for very love of mischief or drove the flat-bottomed punts with long poles through the marshy waters."

"Morin-Premion!" cried Duplessis in amazement.

"And perhaps I can tell how they forced their way to the dense brushwood of the Bocage, or rambled over waste lands covered with broom and furze and of quick-set hedges, and of ox-carts stuck fast in yellow clay, and of the mud-huts of the fishers, and of stolen visits to the salt smugglers in the forest of Concise, and of a thousand things which have to do with this once tranquil La Vendée."

He concluded his discourse by repeating the words of Duplessis in a tone of slight mockery.

"So now, Duplessis, your hand, for old comradeship!"

Duplessis folded his arms upon his breast.

"You would not have refused it once," said Premion, in a tone which was almost suppliant, while his sinister face took on a winning expression, which had already gained him more than one suit in the law courts of Paris.

"No; that I would not!" said Duplessis, assenting to the last remark; "but times change, and men with them, and I must know to what work has been put the hand which I grasp in friendship."

"Mostly to law papers, my friend," said Premion, with a shrug of the shoulders, "though of late, in truth, it has been, perchance, more sternly employed. But what matters that, or why should you presume to think ill of the work I have been doing?"

"If it matches the words I heard from your lips," said Duplessis sturdily, "it is not work which entitles you to grasp my hand in friendship. No, nor the hand of any honest Breton, Christian, and Catholic!"

Premion's brow grew dark with a scowl so lowering that it caused some timid ones, of which there were not many in the ranks of the Breton peasantry, to fall back.

"Have a care, Duplessis," the man cried in a low tone of concentrated rage. "Your late doings are known at Nantes, and the mornings on the marshes will avail you little, nor even the day you drew me from the marsh yonder, if you meet with scorn the friendly advances of a patriot and of a true man."

"True to what?" inquired Duplessis, his honest eyes searching the countenance of the lawyer and his lips obstinately compressed. "To your God, to the traditions of your race, to your pastors, to your faith?"

"True to the nation, to humanity, and its sacred rights," cried Premion, raising his voice, "to liberty, equality, fraternity."

"Keep those ill-omened words for the wine-shops of Paris!" commanded Richard so sternly that the other quailed somewhat before him. "We have learned what true humanity and fraternity are from the lips of our priests, God bless them."

"Aye, God bless them!" echoed the assembly.

"And as to liberty," went on Duplessis, "the peasants of La Vendée have their share. We are free men all, and free we shall remain, mark you, Premion, free to serve our God, unhindered, free to choose our pastors, and free to give our lives for our religion and our King!"

"Bravo! Hurrah!" cried the Vendeans assembled, as with one voice, "Long live the Church, the Pope, the priests, long live the King and our gracious lady, the Queen!" The stranger stood scowling upon them all, his saturnine face growing momentarily more evil in expression. Suddenly there was a change, as though he had drawn a mask over its darkness.

"This is but a sorry welcome for an old friend, Duplessis," he cried, genially; "but let that pass. The day may come when you would right willingly clasp my hand. Meantime, good Citizen Dumartin, bring out your best wine. The company shall drink at my expense. I, Morin-Premion, the Vendean, have gone to Paris, and there lined my pockets by my own wit and industry. Returning, shall I not make merry with my friends?"

There was still some hesitation on the part of the company, but the man's manner was so genial, his countenance so beaming, and his invitation to drink so cordial, that all were presently disarmed, save Duplessis, who, declining with a gesture the wine which Dumartin had brought forth, smoked on in silence. None observed the menacing glance which Morin-Premion from time to time threw at him. That worthy, being now left in possession of the field, set himself to win more and more the good graces of the company. He no longer openly attacked the clergy, the nobles, or the King. But he continued by gesture and innuendo to awaken in the minds of the younger men, at least, an entirely new train of thought. They heard good faith and honesty referred to with a sneer; religion as an excellent safeguard for feminine levity or a corrective for unruly children; new and dazzling opinions, social and political, were clothed in language calculated to hide their dangerous significance.

"Speaking of taxes, my friends," said Premion, in the smooth, fluent tones of the lawyer, "is not the *corvée*, for example, an anachronism in this year of 1793? 'Tis a droll custom, is it not, my friends, when one thinks of it, that we, the commonalty, should mend their roads and keep their bridges safe and see to the foundations of their castles, so that our noble lords may drive upon easy roads in gay coaches, and dwell securely in castles, the threshold of which we may not cross? Eh, Citizen Duplessis, what think you of the *corvée*?"

"What think I of the sky overhead?" answered Duplessis, suddenly raising his penetrating dark eyes to the speaker's face. "There it is, and there it remains."

"You believe, then, that the *corvée* shall remain, that intolerable burden," cried the lawyer, "and that our children's children shall bow their backs to the breaking of stone and the making of roads?"

"Our children's children shall, we hope, bend their necks to the yoke of the Gospel," said Duplessis, "which commands obedience to temporal authority."

Premion laughed.

"You made a mistake, Duplessis," he said, "in not having taken orders. What a preacher you would have been!"

Duplessis flushed, but made no reply.

"In truth," went on the lawyer, "I am merely touching these matters in a light and playful way. *I* shall never break stones nor mend roads; but the wrongs of the commonalty stir me, friends, and I find it hard to sit tamely there, as my good Comrade Duplessis would advise, and endure all tyranny."

"Tyranny as it is used today is an empty word," cried Duplessis. "Or, rather, it is wrongly applied. It is the tyranny of the people that is to be feared, the tyranny of the mob, of the demagogue."

Premion's face darkened to an expression of positive rage, while Duplessis went on scornfully.

"Who has taken away our priests, I ask you, and driven us to worship in fields and caves? Bah! It is revolting. I can not endure the cant of the hour."

"Yes; they have taken away our priests, these republicans," said Dumartin, "and their talk of liberty does not give them back."

"You take things too seriously," said the lawyer; "the priests who have submitted to the Government are the true friends of France, of the people."

"We will have none of them," cried Duplessis, and his words were echoed by the entire assembly.

"Oh, well, oh, well, I spoke hastily," said Premion. "Let us have another glass and talk of pleasant things."

Duplessis, with a hearty good night to the landlord and the other guests, strode from the room, while the wine was brought forth and the talk once more became animated. But Premion no longer touched upon political questions, and there was a perceptible coldness in the manner of Dumartin and many others present.

When all had gone, save one, a man sitting in a distant corner, who seemed to be asleep, and whom Premion supposed to be drunk, the lawyer said suddenly:

"And now, Citizen Dumartin, my worthy landlord and best of innkeepers, that the scratches I received in that unlucky accident are healed, I must leave you tomorrow. I go to Nantes on public business. Therefore, before retiring, I pray you to let me see once more your pearl of a daughter, the lovely Jeanne. I have a token here I would offer her in appreciation of her kindness."

He said the last words in a tone of mockery so studied that it escaped Dumartin's ears.

"Kindness is perchance a strong word," he added presently, with a laugh, "since the fair damsel has not vouchsafed me a word or smile. But I love coyness in the sex, my good Dumartin, and still more do I love beauty, so I would fain offer her my small tribute."

The innkeeper, though his head was somewhat beclouded by a too generous sampling of his own good wine, was manifestly uneasy at the proposal.

"My daughters are abroad, sir. They have been all day with Mademoiselle de Breteuil at the castle."

"The more reason they should be at home now," Premion said in a loud, imperious voice. "It wears late. Send for them, that I may bid them farewell."

The innkeeper, who resented this sudden assumption of authority, and was alarmed at the republican's interest in his daughter, stood uncertain. But at that very moment the door opened and Jeanne, followed by her sister Erminie, entered the room. The two girls stood still at sight of the lawyer in conversation with their father, and Jeanne, with a slight inclination of the head, would have passed upstairs, but Premion stopped her.

"Does a day spent with the aristocrats cause you to forget your manners, my pretty Jeanne?" he asked insolently. "Would it not be better for you to remain here in your proper place, attending to the comfort of your father's guests, than licking the ground under the feet of these nobles, who despise you and us?"

The man was plainly heated by wine, and though Jeanne was naturally courageous, she recoiled a step, while, at the same time, the man who had been sitting in the corner of the room drew near, unperceived by Premion.

"I have told your father that I love beauty," he said, "and have always remembered that face of yours which took my wandering fancy long ago. Some of these days I may raise you up and make you the wife of the celebrated Citizen Premion. How would the title suit you, Citizeness Morin-Premion?"

The man in the cloak, who had drawn near unperceived, turned his back at this moment, as if controlling himself by an effort, while Jeanne's eyes flashed and an angry answer arose to her lips. But she restrained it. Premion was dangerous. If she precipitated a quarrel, the consequences might be terrible. When she spoke, it was coldly, but without apparent irritation.

"You are merry, sir, at my expense. But the jest is a poor one, since I am the betrothed of an honest man!"

"Betrothed!" laughed the lawyer. "In these days, when marriage itself is put aside with other superstitions, a betrothal counts for little."

Then seeing the expression of horror which crossed the faces of the two girls, as they devoutly crossed themselves, Premion changed his tone somewhat.

"Don't look so serious, pretty one, though many a true word is spoken in jest. But tell me, what happy rustic has won your young affections?"

"Richard Duplessis!" answered Jeanne, looking steadily at the lawyer. His face was instantly covered with so dark a scowl that Jeanne repented of having mentioned his name. Indeed, a sudden premonition of evil smote upon her.

"Ah, indeed," said Premion, striving to conceal his anger. "The Citizen Duplessis is scoring well this evening, and I shall not forget him. But bear in mind, my pretty Jeanne, that should a member of the Committee of Public Safety and an officer of the National Vengeance Bureau, one Citizen Premion, seek to elevate you to his own dignity, coyness will have to be put aside, and you will have to meet him with a smile and a 'Thank you, Citizen.'"

"Rather death," muttered Jeanne beneath her breath. The sharp ears of the lawyer caught the exclamation.

"Death in these days comes clad in a crimson garment, my girl, and your neck is too white and slender for Doctor Guillotine's knife. Therefore, be warned in time, and accept this trifling souvenir which I offer you as an earnest of what you may expect."

He held out a small box wherein lay a jeweled ring, flashing from its velvet setting in the firelight which leaped up from the hearth.

Jeanne made no movement to take it, and Premion observed, "You, who are so fond of aristocrats, may prize the bauble the more, that it belonged to a Countess, who, proving herself an enemy of the people, was beheaded last week."

With a sharp cry of horror, Jeanne, followed by her sister, flew past the lawyer and upstairs to her own apartment, while her father, his brain beclouded by wine, still stood, stupidly staring, pipe in mouth, as if only partly comprehending what was going forward. And the man in the cloak, who had attentively followed the conversation, slipped out of the room, still unobserved, and rushed stumbling on through the darkness.

He stopped at a substantial farm building, which stood somewhat back from the highway, and knocked at the door. The door was instantly opened by Richard Duplessis himself.

"Is it you, Henriot?" he inquired, shading his eyes with his hand.

"Yes, Maître Duplessis, 'tis I!"

"You heard what was said after I had left the inn?"

"I did, and am here to bring you news of it."

Duplessis drew him within, and having carefully closed the door, listened with compressed lips and frowning brow to the tale which the other had to tell.

"And so, Morin-Premion," he cried, clenching his fists, "you have come as the hawk from the feast of carrion below at the Capital to fasten on the dove."

"Why did you not leave him to rot on the road when his carriage was overturned?" grumbled Henriot, who was none other than the servant of Count Gaston de la Roche André, eldest son of the Marquis of that name, and the feudal seigneur of the parish of Saint Lyphar.

"Nay, lad!" he cried. "I knew nothing of him or his character when I undertook to play the good Samaritan. You would not have had me pass on the other side?"

"I would have had you not go near the place at all," said Henriot, decidedly. He was not very clear as to who or what was the good Samaritan. "And now I must hasten to tell them at the castle what kind of fowl is roosting at the Red Inn."

"Do not alarm Madame," urged Duplessis. "Nor yet Mademoiselle de Breteuil. She is an angel, a beautiful spirit. She must not be soiled with the touch of pitch."

"But Monsieur le Marquis?" inquired Henriot.

"It is well he should know," said Duplessis, thoughtfully. "But I am glad Monsieur Gaston is not here. Premion is dangerous."

"You are already in his black books!" declared Henriot.

"That matters nothing at all," cried Duplessis, with a shrug. "But it is best that yonder vulture know nothing of our knowledge. He must not suppose that I heard of his language to——"

He turned away in anger. It choked him to think of his beautiful Jeanne subjected to such an ordeal.

"'Tis for that I have played rat!" said Henriot. "He believed me drunk or imbecile."

He chuckled as he drew his hat over his eyes and prepared to set out for the castle, but Duplessis stopped him.

"It is very likely that Count Gaston will be here soon, for look you, Henriot," and the young man drew a folded paper from his breast, "Jambe d'Argent has given us rendezvous at the inn."

Henriot, who could not read, waited till Duplessis disclosed to him the contents of the paper:

"'In the holy name of God, on the King's behalf, the parish of Saint Lyphar is invited to send as many men as possible to the Camp of the High Meadows, a week hence, at seven o'clock of the night.'

"Count Gaston is to meet me tomorrow at midnight in the parlor of the Red Inn."

"Count Gaston," exclaimed Henriot, turning very pale.

"He will be there!" said Duplessis, quietly, "with sealed orders from Jambe d'Argent himself. After our conference, nothing will remain but the camp and the field."

"God help all we love, Maître Duplessis," said Henriot in a low voice.

"In Him we put our trust," answered Duplessis, solemnly.

A moment after Henriot was speeding homeward to the castle, and Duplessis, left alone, paced the room in uncontrollable agitation.

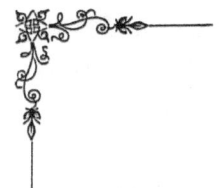
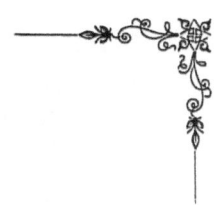

Chapter II

Madame Confers With Richard Duplessis

NOW THAT THE STORM was gathering about the heads of the nobility, it behooved the faithful peasants of Saint Lyphar to show their devoted attachment to the family of their feudal lords, the illustrious house of La Roche André. Hence, on that lovely autumnal morning which followed the somber night at the Red Inn, when Madame made her appearance in the village streets, the people were all eagerness to show their respect, their good will, their devoted attachment. It saddened them to behold her, clad in funereal black, for the news from Paris had been bad, and Madame's brother, an officer of artillery, had lost his life in the service of his King during the storming of the Bastile. Madame's sweet face was none the less serene and smiling. She was of a race which met death with a smile when it befell at the post of duty, and she accounted it an honor that her kinsman should have fallen in defense of all that he held sacred.

As she passed on her way, conversing with her dearly loved people, each of whom she saluted by name, the villagers crowded about, the men hat in hand, bowing low, women teaching their children to make pretty speeches to the great and beautiful lady from the castle yonder. There was nothing slavish or servile in the love and respect of these simple Vendeans for their superior. They were free with the true liberty of the children of God, while the nobles of that district, on their side, regarded their dependents with a patriarchal, almost paternal, interest. Madame was truly their mother.

They could have recourse to her in all their trials, as Monsieur le Marquis was their protector against all aggressors, and the gallant young Gaston their outspoken champion.

Madame had come down to the village to inform herself concerning this wolf in sheep's clothing who had come into the fold, striving to disseminate his perfidious opinions among her people. She had all the scorn, a trifle narrow, perhaps, of the true noble for such opinions and those who held them. But among the ignorant those counsels of evil might prevail, faith be weakened, charity lessened, envy excited. Moreover, Jeanne had been threatened, that pretty, innocent Jeanne, who had been the devoted companion of Madame's ward and future daughter-in-law, Yseult de Breteuil. Jeanne must be protected. This ill-omened traveler must not be permitted to gain a foothold in the village.

When Madame reached the Red Inn, she found Jeanne pale and with a troubled look in her eyes. The girl's intuitions warned her that there was real danger in the admiration of such a man as Morin-Premion, and she felt that he had the power to support his pretensions in a manner disastrous to Richard Duplessis and to her own happiness. These misgivings she freely confided to Madame.

"But, my child, the Blessed Mother will protect you," Madame said; "have recourse to her. She can gain all from her divine Son, and as to earthly protectors, you have Monsieur le Marquis and your good friend, Count Gaston, who would cut off his right hand rather than that harm should come to his former playmate. Then, of course, there is that other, the brave and handsome Duplessis. Ah, there you are blushing, and it is well—the blushes of a first innocent love are very beautiful, and not to be hidden."

There was a sadness in Madame's face as she pressed the young girl's hand.

"I am so glad," she went on, "that your father has chosen so wisely, and that your heart is with the choice. I know of no one so worthy of our Jeanne as this Duplessis. He has a noble heart, my child, and great strength of character. So fear not."

"It is for him I fear," said Jeanne, in a low, trembling voice. "O Madame, had you seen the look upon that bad man's face when I mentioned Richard's name."

Madame looked grave.

"It is true," she said, "that a viper may sting the noblest and the strongest. But you tell me this man is gone now, and he must not come back. Mark you, Dumartin," she added, raising her voice to include the innkeeper, "this Premion must not come back."

"Madame," answered Dumartin, "not with my will; but he is of the Committee of Public Safety and of the National Vengeance, too. Alas! he can come and go when he will! Aye, and have us all carried off, too, if it so please him."

It still seemed as a dream to the handsome and high-spirited lady of rank that there should be any other power in that region than that of Monsieur le Marquis, and either individuals or organizations which could dare defy that power.

"I do not think he will venture very far," she said, with that same easy carelessness as to the future and want of provision which marked the governing classes at the time of the Revolution; "for, let me see, was not the father of this Premion Monsieur's swineherd?"

"Yes, Madame," answered Dumartin; "and this very lad himself tended the swine. But, alas, times have changed. He is a lawyer now, come to this district on public business, and a member of the Committee of Public Safety. Ah, Madame, no one is safe with whom that Committee has to do."

"I believe you are right there," said Madame; "the Committee of Public Safety very much endangers the safety of every one."

Neither the innkeeper nor his daughter echoed the laugh. It seemed to them as if this fair and smiling lady, fair despite her two grown up sons, one of whom was with the army and the other at the College of Vannes, and smiling despite the impending ruin, stood upon a mine which might at any moment explode. Dumartin, who, over night confused by wine, had realized little of what was happening, was now full of misgivings.

"Send for Duplessis," said the Marquise, suddenly, impressed, perhaps, by the gravity of the two. "I would like to hear his opinion."

Richard came presently, bowing low to the Marquise, who held out her hand to him with a charming smile.

"I want to talk to you of many things," she said, "but chiefly of what concerns one whom you hold dear."

"It is of Jeanne Madame would speak," Duplessis answered frankly, flushing slightly as he spoke.

"Precisely; the poor little heart is much cast down this morning, and all because of you."

Madame held Jeanne's hand while she spoke.

"Because of me?" Duplessis inquired in surprise. Then he remembered, and added hastily: "She fears the demagogue who was here last night, the fighter of shadows, the republican."

"Yes," said Madame; "she fears Morin-Premion."

"And justly!" murmured Duplessis, adding aloud: "Would Madame favor me with a moment's private speech? I have something to communicate."

Madame released Jeanne's hand.

"Go, my pretty one," she said.

"But for a moment," whispered Richard in Jeanne's ear.

"You should have no secrets from me," protested Jeanne; "we need each other in these evil times."

"Trust me, Jeanne, *ma chérie*, my beloved one!" cried Duplessis. "It is best that I speak with Madame alone."

Jeanne smiled at him. She admired the touch of authority in his look and tone. He would be wise for both of them in the coming times, as he was already brave and strong.

"You are always right, Richard!" she cried, impulsively, hurrying away to where her father was already busy with a customer

17

in the room adjoining. The Marquise, left alone with Duplessis, began at once:

"She fears Premion, and justly, you say?"

"It is never wise to underestimate a danger," Duplessis said gravely; "and the man is certainly all powerful for evil."

"It is for you she fears," Madame observed quietly.

"For me?" Duplessis laughed.

"And yet she is right. As a man he might be powerless against you." And Madame, while she spoke, looked admiringly at the young man's strong and sinewy proportions. "But as a member of the Safety, of the Vengeance——"

"I must take all chances, as better men have done, Madame," Duplessis answered; "but for Jeanne, the danger is imminent. If there is any place you can advise, I would have her sent away, and this brings me to a delicate matter."

The young man was visibly embarrassed.

"Speak, Duplessis," said the Marquise kindly.

"What I have to say refers to a member of your own household."

A shadow fell upon the bright face of the listener, as a cloud upon the surface of a shining lake.

"Speak, nevertheless!" she cried, with a certain tone of command, of pride, as though declaring herself equal to all misfortunes.

"This Premion, this miscreant," said Duplessis, hesitating no longer, "has been heard to say that he would marry Jeanne tomorrow, in spite of the whole parish, were it not that his admiration is divided. In short, he has dared to bring in the name of Mademoiselle de Breteuil."

"Enough," said Madame; "I understand!"

She was very pale and silent for a moment, during which Richard kept his eyes steadily fixed upon the somber Breton landscape, visible from the latticed window of the inn. Then Madame spoke:

"His very utterance of their names insults the innocence of our beloved ones, but you are right. When he has ventured so far, they must be placed at once outside the circle of his infamous influence. There is a convent in Bas Poitou where, for the time being, they shall be safe. I shall inform Monsieur without delay. They must go as soon as possible. It is fortunate that Count Gaston is absent. For, in spite of all consequences, this wretch's bones would be broken."

"I have contributed to that end myself," said Duplessis. "This morning, as he was leaving for Nantes, I chanced to meet him at a point just beyond the village, and I broke a stick upon him. It was a stout stick, too. He returned to the Public Safety in a damaged state."

There was a grim smile of satisfaction upon his face as he spoke, but Madame cried out in terror:

"Oh, you have been imprudent. You have put your life in danger."

"I am a man," said Duplessis, quietly, "and having heard what passed last night, I could not permit him to go unpunished. His insults to my betrothed wife and his insolent mention of that other name demanded chastisement. While revenging my own wrongs, I had a thought for Monsieur Gaston, too. So I gave him a double share."

The Marquise, despite her anxiety, could not repress a smile.

"I am afraid it is a bad business for you," she observed.

"Had I followed my own inclination, Madame," said Duplessis, "I should have killed him. I had to remember that I was a Catholic and a Vendean, and that murder is a crime."

"Jeanne will be always sure of a protector while that right arm is free," said Madame, sadly. "But, oh, there are manacles for the stoutest arms and dungeons for the bravest hearts."

"Once Jeanne and that other are safe," declared the young man, "I shall take the risk. In any case, I shall be leaving Saint Lyphar in the course of the week. For," and he lowered his voice, and glanced cautiously toward the door, "the summons has come from Jambe d'Argent for the men of the parish."

Madame leaned back in her chair, pressing her hand to her heart.

"So soon," she murmured; "so soon."

"I meet Count Gaston tonight," Duplessis went on.

"Where?"

"Here at the Red Inn. Count Gaston will be here."

"Gaston here!" cried the Marquise, sitting upright, and drawing a quick, gasping breath, then, almost immediately, she added: "Of course, I might have known it. Who should lead the men of Saint Lyphar except their natural chief? Monsieur le Marquis is too old. Gaston must take his place."

"I need not remind you, Madame," said Duplessis, "that it is of the last importance that his coming be kept secret. He brings our orders. I shall serve under him as his lieutenant."

"The closest secrecy shall be enforced!" said Madame. "Only ourselves and Henriot must know of his coming. Meantime, beware, lest this Premion should seize upon your person."

"Once this meeting is over," said Duplessis, "I can treat him, if necessary, to a game of *cache-cache*. He could never catch me in those old days in the marshes and the Bocage."

He smiled and the Marquise looked at him with almost the same admiration she would have bestowed upon her beloved Gaston.

"And now as to Mademoiselle and Jeanne," she said, controlling the emotion which had been awakened by the thought of Gaston's arrival and of the new dangers which threatened him. "I shall learn Monsieur's pleasure in that matter without delay. A gentleman of Poitou, who is at present our guest, M. de Kergarion, will be returning home in a day or two, and I shall place our dear ones under his safe conduct. He will see them within the convent walls. I will speak to Dumartin at once."

"And I will prepare Jeanne," agreed Duplessis.

"Will she listen to you?"

"I have an infallible argument. I shall tell her that as regards Premion, her absence will best insure my safety, and, moreover, that

I can with a free mind devote myself to the service of God and the King when I know that she is sheltered from harm."

"May God protect us all," sighed the Marquise.

"Amen," said the soldier of La Vendée, reverently bowing his head.

"For, oh, Duplessis," cried the lady, with sudden weakening, "I begin to see, to feel all. Evil times are upon us, and the end is not yet."

"God will be our helper; God and our Lady," said Duplessis, solemnly; "but the time is come when some of us must take up arms again for our faith and our King, for God and country. Adieu, Madame."

And Duplessis turned away as if to conceal his emotion, while Madame, looking after him, murmured:

"Thank God that in La Vendée, at least, there are many such as he!"

Upon her return to the chateau, she related all that had passed to the Marquis. He was so deeply affected by the intelligence that he seemed unable to think or speak of anything else. So that when Madame sat upon the terrace with M. de Kergarion, her guest, listening to the news of events in Paris, which had been brought by two young gentlemen of Poitou, who had called to pay their respects to the family of La Roche André, the Marquis paced back and forth in solitary meditation. He was a man of quick and penetrating intellect, and already he perceived, as in a panorama spread out before him, the blood-stained land of France. He already seemed to see the smoke from the chateaux, the dismal processions to the guillotine, and the extinguished lights upon the altar, and it came to him with overpowering sadness, the futility of effort. He knew that already the peasants of La Vendée, under Stofflet and Cathelineau, under Larochejaquelein and Lescuri, had measured their strength with the republican forces, and in many instances had borne away the palm of victory. But such victories, he well knew, were elusive, and but the ignis fatuus which lured the insurgents on to ultimate ruin. He had no doubt whatever of the justice of their cause, nor did he desire for one moment that they should relinquish the struggle and submit without effort to the new conditions. On the contrary, it was his intention to be present at the meeting of leaders in the parlor of the Red Inn, and there to encourage, by every means in his power, this movement among his people. Since his age prevented him from going with them to the ranks of the Catholic and royal army, he would, at least, share the risks of their secret deliberations, and offer his son to be the leader of the enterprise. He fully agreed, however, with Madame, that their ward, the beautiful Yseult de Breteuil, the daughter of an old friend, and, as they hoped, the future wife of their eldest son, Count Gaston, should no longer remain in a neighborhood which might be constantly polluted by the presence of the unprincipled demagogue, Premion. And as he walked thus and pondered on all these things, he heard one of the young men on the terrace say:

"That rascally Premion, one of the most base of Carrier's infernal crew, has been laid up by the heels. An honest royalist, it appears, gave him the beating he has long deserved. I say, Long live that royalist, whoever he be."

"But," objected the brother, "that good action may cost the Vendean dear. For Premion has sworn to send him to the guillotine in less than a month with his sweetheart, who, it seems, has abetted the royalist, and that he himself will smoke out a certain nest of aristocrats, and, having married a certain lady of rank, will settle down quietly in the untenanted chateau."

The young man rattled all this news out carelessly. He had no idea that it was in Saint Lyphar Premion had been beaten, nor that any of the actors in the drama he had just outlined could be known to the household of Roche André. What was his consternation, then, when he saw Madame fall back in her chair, pale and half fainting, while the Marquis, startled by the exclamations of M. de Kergarion and the two young men, hurried to the spot. He, too, had heard the fatal words, and guessed the reason of his wife's seizure. By a great effort Madame presently rallied.

"It is nothing, gentlemen," she said; "a slight weakness. I have been overfatiguing myself today, walking to and from the village."

For she did not wish that these young men, gentlemen though they were and royalists, should connect the family of Roche André and the name of Yseult de Breteuil with the odious official of the revolutionary tribunals. She led the conversation easily and lightly into safer channels, and it was only after the young men had taken their leave and M. de Kergarion had retired to his apartments that she discussed the matter with her husband.

"You heard what was said of Premion?" she inquired of her husband, with trembling eagerness.

"Yes; and though I can not bring myself to regret what our brave Duplessis has done—it was the natural impulse of an honest man—I feel sure that Premion will, if possible, carry out his threat. He can easily find matter of accusation for Duplessis's gallant behavior with Cathelineau, and his grand army have already made him a marked man."

"But it was not only Duplessis whom he threatened," faltered Madame.

"I know, he has ventured much further," said the Marquis, trying to control the anger which boiled up within him. "Mademoiselle de Breteuil, with the little Dumartin, shall proceed with M. de Kergarion tomorrow or next day to the convent. After that we shall see if the men of Roche André can not deal with this scoundrel as he deserves."

He paced up and down the room, adding presently: "You will forgive the warmth of my expressions, and as for Yseult, she must hear nothing, save that the country is disturbed."

"God forbid that she should hear anything more," said Madame; "it is bad enough that poor, pretty Jeanne should learn from the man himself of his insulting admiration; but our Yseult, never."

"We allude to the matter for the last time, my love," said the Marquis. "M. de Kergarion travels with two or three mounted servants, well armed. We need have no further fear. But I need not remind you that meantime Yseult must not stir outside the grounds."

And so it was settled that the two girls should go away. Richard, as he had promised, broke the news to Jeanne, who had answered bravely:

"It breaks my heart to leave you, Richard, for the few days that you will be in Saint Lyphar. But if it is for your safety, I would go to the end of the world. And, O, Richard, tell me truly, shall you be safe?"

"I shall be looked after, do you see, by the Committee of Public Safety," laughed Richard.

"You are jesting when my heart is sore within me," said Jeanne, reproachfully.

"But there is no reason for heartache, little sweetheart," said Richard, "except that we shall be separated, and that we should have been in any case, as I must follow Monsieur Gaston to the camp of Jambe d'Argent. Once there, I shall not give much heed to the Blues."

"Promise me, my dearest, that you will not in the mean time quarrel with this terrible Premion."

"There is no immediate danger of a quarrel," said Duplessis with a smile, thinking with satisfaction that Premion would not be in good fighting condition for some time to come.

"Promise me!" persisted Jeanne.

"Well, I am not likely to attack Premion," said Richard, "and I don't think he will attack me."

"That is no promise."

"If he attacks me, I suppose I must defend myself," Richard answered, still laughing, but there was an infinite tenderness in his tone, as he added: "Dry those tears, my true-hearted Jeanne, my own dearest love. Be comforted, the man for the moment is powerless."

Jeanne was called away just then by a message from Mademoiselle de Breteuil, begging that she would go up to the castle. Yseult ran to meet her.

"Did you know that we are going away together to the Convent at Thouars?"

"Yes, Mademoiselle," Jeanne answered sadly.

"You must not call me Mademoiselle, and you must not pull such a long face. As for me, I am always delighted to see my dear nuns. But I wonder why we are being sent."

"I know why I am being sent," cried Jeanne, with flashing eyes. "It is because of a wretch who has come to our village, and who insults me with his admiration."

"How romantic," exclaimed Yseult, "and how vexed your handsome Richard must have been. But what was this man like?"

"Tall, with a brown beard and black eyes that snapped when he talked."

"O," said Yseult, with sudden remembrance, "I think I have seen him, too."

And then she grew very thoughtful, remembering, with a shudder, the face of a man who had insolently stared at her over the wall of the flower-garden some days before, and who had dared to call out:

"Beautiful as Diana. The queen of the flowers herself!"

Her face crimsoned at the recollection, but she would not speak of such a thing.

"Were Count Gaston to hear of it," she thought; "but, thank God, he never shall."

The thought was followed by another. She was a girl of wonderfully clear insight. The man was causing Jeanne's banishment by his insulting notice. Could he have dared to bring her own name into his revolting speech?

"You will help me, Jeanne, to prepare," she said quietly. "M. de Kergarion has decided to leave tomorrow, and, for my part, I am anxious to be gone."

"You do not know, then," said Jeanne, somewhat nettled by Yseult's eagerness to leave Saint Lyphar, "that Count Gaston will arrive tonight?"

A lovely color glowed in Yseult's cheeks. She was so beautiful, with her oval face, refined and spiritual, her sensitive nature, full of unexpected depths, of outreaching sympathy. For a moment her imagination pictured the handsome, glowing face of the young Count, all eagerness, riding up the avenue in his dark blue riding-coat and three-cornered hat, as she had last seen him. She could almost hear his voice, so clear and ringing, so vibrant and passionate at times, when stirred by any emotion.

"I did not know, I had not heard!" she said, with some hesitation.

"His coming is a secret, which I, perhaps, had no right to reveal," said Jeanne. "It is on public business."

"On public business?" repeated Yseult, bewildered.

"He will not come to the castle."

"Where, then?"

"To the parlor of the Red Inn, and at midnight. The men of Saint Lyphar have been summoned. He is to lead them, with Richard as his lieutenant."

Yseult's eyes opened wide with a look of fear and horror, her face grew pale, her lips trembled.

"He has been in danger already," she said, "in battle; but this is different. O my God!"

And she covered her face with her hands.

"I have told you this," said Jeanne, in a firm voice, though her face, too, reflected something of the other's anguish, "because I thought you might like to see and bid him farewell."

Yseult drew back with a hasty movement.

"You mistake," she said, proudly. "We are not betrothed. He has not yet asked formally for my hand. I can not go to meet him."

"Mademoiselle," said Jeanne, "we peasants treat our hearts better than you nobles. Monsieur Gaston loves you, worships the very ground you tread upon. The betrothal is delayed only because of this war. He will not come to the castle for fear of endangering your safety. He will not ask you to meet him for the same reason. But you are going away, and he, in a week's time, will be in the van of the Catholic army. I, a peasant, would not hesitate to bid him Godspeed, at least. You, as a lady, must do as you will!"

There was a severe struggle going on in Yseult's mind. Jeanne's words struck her to the heart, as a dagger might have done, and yet there were pride, reserve, the traditions of her caste, the very opinion which Gaston might form of her conduct, all warring against that one desire to bid her young soldier farewell and encourage him by her own words to fight the good fight for King and country.

"I will go," she said at last, "to the Red Inn, for a quarter of an hour, before the midnight meeting. You and Erminie will attend me, and you will accompany me back to the chateau. Let it be understood that my desire is to encourage, by personal sympathy, the chief of this movement and his lieutenant."

Jeanne looked at her with surprise. She could not understand.

"So long as you come, it is well," she said. "But forgive my plain speaking, Mademoiselle, the love of an honest heart need not be hidden under fine phrases."

"Let it suffice that I have promised to come to the Red Inn tonight," said Yseult, with some haughtiness, and so they parted.

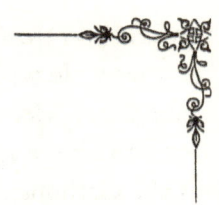

Chapter III

A Spy Appears in the Neighborhood of the Red Inn

HEN Yseult de Breteuil had promised Jeanne that she would visit the Red Inn at the hour appointed for the conference between Count Gaston and his lieutenant, she had resolved to say nothing of her determination to the Marquis and Marquise de la Roche André. Though she was not aware of their special anxiety on her account, because of the boastful talk of the parvenu lawyer, she felt certain that they would disapprove of the risk she was running. Moreover, she shrank not a little from announcing to them a project which was far from being in consonance with her reserve of character and the traditions of her caste.

On the other hand, Jeanne's argument had powerfully affected her. The sturdy common sense and womanliness of the peasant-bred girl had brushed aside, like a cobweb, what was, after all, a mere convention. Gaston was her playmate, her early friend, almost her brother. He was going into the heart of a desperate struggle, and he was even risking his life by this secret visit to Saint Lyphar, where the organization peculiar to the forces of one leader, the celebrated Jambe d'Argent, was already in existence. For by means of this system the men of the village remained at home, in readiness, however, for instant service under their natural leaders. Gaston was facing death for the noblest of all causes. Should she not, therefore, show her sympathy with that movement, and a sister's interest in the man who was its local representative?

Therefore, she managed to leave the castle, in company with Jeanne, who had met her at the gate, proceeding with as much caution and secrecy as possible to the Red Inn of Saint Lyphar. Muffled in their cloaks, so as to be almost entirely unrecognizable, the two girls were admitted to the inn by Erminie and conducted at once to a small apartment adjoining the tap-room, where a man, seated at a table, seemed lost in deep thought. Yseult did not at first recognize Gaston, whom she had never seen before in the costume of La Vendée.

He wore a short, gray surcoat, tied with blue, a white woolen waistcoat, and breeches of brown wool. On the table beside him was a broad-brimmed hat, adorned with a white cockade and an oaken sprig. From his buttonhole was suspended a rosary, while a scapular at his breast was a further token of his enlistment in the Catholic and royal army.

He turned sharply round at the opening of the door, and as Yseult threw back her cloak, he sprang to his feet.

"Mademoiselle," he cried, in a tone of so great astonishment that Yseult felt her face crimson. In an instant, however, her natural dignity came to her aid.

"Monsieur Gaston," she said, "I have learned that you are here on a perilous mission, and that you are going hence to the camp of the insurgent leader. Since such is the case, considering our early friendship, I could not let you go without a word of farewell."

"Mademoiselle," said Gaston, and his manner, at once grave and ceremonious, put the young girl more at her ease than anything else could have done, "I am deeply touched by a thoughtfulness on your part, which will ease the pain of my departure and brighten the future before me."

Then with a sudden involuntary outburst:

"O, Yseult, you have put your life in danger, and for me."

The girl turned aside, full of an indescribable emotion, but instantly Gaston resumed his former grave courtesy of look and tone.

He would sooner have cut off his right hand than have reminded her at that moment of the tender relations which he hoped would one day unite them. She had come as a sister. It was the part of a gentleman to maintain the fraternal relation.

"You know, perhaps, that I am about to leave the chateau," Yseult said, breaking the somewhat embarrassing silence.

"I had not known it!" cried Gaston in surprise. "It must be very sudden."

"Jeanne and I are being put in shelter in a convent."

"You will be safe there, it is true," said Gaston, thoughtfully. "But why this sudden decision on my father's part? The chateau has not been threatened? You have not been annoyed in any manner?"

Yseult felt the hot blood mounting to her face. She could not bear the thought that Gaston should know of Premion's insolent braggadocio.

"Your father says it is a measure of precaution," Yseult answered, "resolved upon in solemn conclave of our elders."

Gaston gave her a keen look. He was not deceived by the lightness of her tone and words. But he did not push the inquiry any further.

"So that is another reason I wanted to see you and say farewell, and to let you know how perfectly I am in sympathy with the cause. O, Gaston, it is a glorious thing to fight for God and the King."

How beautiful she was thus, with her glowing cheeks and eyes lighted by a sacred enthusiasm! Gaston felt that at that moment he fairly worshiped her with all the ardor of his glowing Celtic nature. But he only said sadly:

"You forget we have no King any more."

"But we shall have. It is his cause none the less, the cause of royalty."

"And now," said Gaston, "the brother is about to assert his authority and bid you return to the chateau without delay. It grieves me, for your own sake, that I dare not accompany you, lest any spy should follow and denounce us."

"Jeanne will accompany me," said Yseult gaily. "She is guard sufficient."

"She shall come to no harm, I promise you, Monsieur Gaston, that I can prevent," spoke up Jeanne, sturdily, from the position near the door where she and Erminie, at Yseult's request, had stationed themselves.

"To you, then, I confide her," he said, turning to Jeanne, with that gracious affability which so endeared him to the commonalty.

"Adieu, Mademoiselle," he said, taking Yseult's hand. "Let me offer you the certainty of a devotion which shall never fail. I shall never forget tonight, and, perhaps, you will never know what inspiration I have found in your words and presence here."

"Godspeed you and your gallant cause, Gaston!" cried Yseult. "May He have you in His keeping till we meet again!"

Then, without another word, she signed to Jeanne to follow, and left the Red Inn.

On the days following the meeting between Count Gaston and Duplessis, the details of which were kept secret save to those concerned, there was a strange flutter in the village. Secret preparations were being carried on at all the farms and in the mud cabins of the peasantry. News from the Capital, from Nantes, from Angers, was coming in by every post; strange, wild news which seemed to these peasants incredible. The nation was in a ferment, and La Vendée was already taking part in the universal upheaval. Movements were everywhere on foot, victories had been won over the Blues, and peasants and gentlemen were fighting, or preparing to fight, side by side for King, for country, but more than all, for the grand old faith dear to their Gaelic hearts. Men might die for what they would, the soldiers of La Vendée would die first of all for God. And this gave them a heroic valor, an endurance, a determination, incomprehensible to the republicans. The names of Larochejaquelein,

Lescuri, Cathelineau, Stofflet, d'Elbée and Bonchamp were even then on every tongue, while Charette, Jean Chouan de Puissage, and a dozen other intrepid leaders were later to give their lives for the cause of God.

The parishes were gradually organizing, or had already organized, and, having driven off the Blues, the peasants returned to their farms, calmly pursued their work, and waited for a fresh summons to arms.

At Saint Lyphar a light snow had fallen, yet the streets were thronged with women assembling in anxious groups. It was known that Monsieur Gaston had come home, riding gaily up to the castle, no longer in the homespun of the Catholic army, but in the richest apparel possible, and riding with him had come his brother, the serious and silent student from the College at Vannes. Count Gaston's object in appearing thus openly at his father's ancestral dwelling was to divert suspicion from his secret movements, until the plans which he and Duplessis had formed could be perfected. But it served to mystify still further the simple villagers, and especially the kindred of those who had enlisted in the royalist army. It was further known that Mademoiselle de Breteuil, accompanied by Jeanne Dumartin, had left Saint Lyphar for a place of greater safety.

Hence the feeling of uneasiness which was abroad. The Red Inn itself had an air almost of desolation, so thought the Marquis de la Roche André as he came thither on the third morning after the secret meeting. None stood about the door save Richard Duplessis, who, with grave and care-shadowed face, conversed with Erminie. The Marquis paused and looked awhile at the house. Its aspect seemed to him to speak already of change and desolation. How gay it used to look, with the red firelight streaming out through door and window, and old Dumartin welcoming his guests with beaming face to his hospitable place of entertainment. The Marquis, never a man of many words, saluted Duplessis with unusual gravity. Erminie, engrossed in the topic uppermost in her mind, of her beloved sister, never even observed the approach of the old gentleman until he had gone by.

The whole atmosphere chilled and depressed the Marquis, and he passed on with head bent and measured step. He was quite unaware that a man in the background observed his every movement, and seemed particularly anxious to know if he entered the Red Inn or held any communication with its inmates. The fellow, who was dressed in striped trousers, with waistcoat of calico, coat of brown wool, with a woolen cap upon his head, and who was evidently a stranger in the parish, did not at once perceive Duplessis or his companion, who were hidden by a projection of the inn wall. Nor might he have perceived them at all, so intent was he upon his observations, had not Duplessis addressed him in stern, decided accents:

"Friend, have you any business with the Marquis de la Roche André."

The spy started and appeared for the moment crestfallen and subdued. Presently he recovered himself, and with the swaggering gait and tone which were the hall marks of the revolutionists answered:

"I deny your right to question me; but if your ears itch for information, I have a curiosity to see the Citizen Roche André, who is in bad repute where I come from as a harborer of priests and the father of at least one red-hot traitor to the nation."

Duplessis repressed his anger as best he could.

"Keep your vile tavern talk for where it will be relished, or your ears may suffer, my fine cockatoo, and you may chance to get a bath in the Loire."

"Here is a fine nest of traitors," said the spy, recoiling a pace or two. "We, the friends of the nation, will have to smoke it out. And you, Citizen, have a care, or you may dance to Madame Guillotine's singing."

"Traitor to your teeth, vile dog of a spy!" cried Richard, losing all control of himself, as he realized that the man before him was, no doubt, one of those infamous "spies of the mountain" who were just then tracking suspected persons and committing all manner of crimes in the neighborhood of Nantes. He would very possibly have fallen upon the fellow and given him a thrashing had not the calm, grave voice of the Marquis interposed. He had turned back at the sound of angry voices.

"My brave Duplessis, control yourself!" he said; "your hands were made for better work. And you, fellow, give an account of yourself, and your business here."

Fire flashed from the Marquis' eyes, and his was a terrible voice of authority when pitched to anger.

"I have overheard your discourse," he said, "which assuredly can not be allowed in this district. If you have not left Saint Lyphar in an hour, I shall cause my servants to use their staves upon you, and, believe me, the beating you shall then receive will be in proportion to your offense. Therefore, be warned in time, and depart while your skin is whole."

The fellow slunk away, awed as much by the majesty of the old man as by his threats. He knew enough of the place to be certain that the commands of the Marquis would be faithfully carried out, and he had little relish for a drubbing from the servants of Roche André. When, however, the Marquis had passed on and the spy was at a safe distance from Duplessis and the inn, he stopped and shook his fist threateningly, sending a whole shower of imprecations after the venerable figure.

"He shall soon lie low, shorter by a head, though I did not catch the cunning old fox in communication with the traitors of the inn. He little knows that I, hidden in the top room, heard every word that was said by his traitor of a son to the villain Duplessis. Aye, and more than that." And the fellow laughed at the recollection.

"I saw the girl from the castle up yonder come a sweethearting with the young Roche André, and she put her neck into my hands, too, with her talk about the Catholic army. Premion wants her for himself, some say, though others will tell you that he prefers the peasant, Dumartin. If that be so, maybe this aristocrat might be knocked to me. No, no; what a fine thing is revolution."

He danced for very glee, adding presently, however, with a darkening countenance:

"And as for this fine Duplessis, Premion will pay well for the news I have to tell of him. If I can but reach Nantes in time, the journey he takes will not be to Jambe d'Argent's camp, but to the dungeon of the Clock Tower. After that the national razor will soon lop off his accursed head."

He laughed aloud again in his gratification at the prospect.

"Oh, but there will be a dance when all these fat peasants, who have put down their names as recruits for the brigands, shall be sent to build the underground fort of the Loire or shot in the quarries of Gigant. But who comes? I must keep out of sight." He stepped into a doorway which stood invitingly open, and whence he looked cautiously forth. It was Madame la Marquise de la Roche André, who came down the village street, accompanied by her two sons. She was, indeed, a proud and joyful mother as she walked between the two stalwart young men. Robert, the younger, had but just left the College at Vannes with a view to joining the army, and Gaston, her *preux* chevalier, had already won honors in the field. He had served with the Royal Regiment, and had been present at Versailles at that fatal but heroic banquet, when the last, wild enthusiasm of loyal hearts expended itself in vivats and cheering. Gaston had vividly described to his mother the inspiring moment when the band had struck up *"Richard, O mon Roi,"* and, amid a storm of applause, the gentlemen present had sprung to their feet, drinking a toast to Louis, the King, and to the Queen, who just then appeared holding her son in her arms. Gaston still proudly wore the white cockade which the Queen had pinned upon the breast of every officer and noble present, but he had long since exchanged the brilliant uniform of the Royal Regiment, now no longer in existence, for the gray frieze of the Vendean army, and had followed the fortunes of d'Elbée and Bonchamp.

So the heart of Madame beat with pride in her sons, and particularly this handsome Gaston. In their honor she had cast aside the mourning garb and appeared, as of old, in a costly robe made by a modiste of the Capital, and a mantle of rich velvet. The spy, from his hiding-place, could hear the village children whispering that this was the beautiful Marquise, and the two great gentlemen her sons. Gaston, in particular, was the idol of every village youth. They told of the honors he had won, of his bravery, of his splendid uniform and sword which he had been accustomed to wear, and of the feats of arms he had performed. He was to them as a legendary hero of old tales, and the wretch, who listened, ground his teeth with malignant envy at the good looks, the good fortune, the high station, and the popularity of the young soldier. He was, in truth, dear to the hearts of the people as their native land itself, the beloved young Count, their champion, who had fought many a battle for the weaker ones of the village, who had relieved so much misery and shown himself always gallant and chivalrous, generous and full of kindness toward the poor. In religion he had been their exemplar. In the courtesy of a gentleman of ancient lineage he had been without a peer, and the simplicity and elegance of his manners had won for him distinction at a court which had been the most brilliant in Europe. Robert, the younger of the two, was less known to the people, having been long absent at college, and was less likely to attain popularity than his brother, being of a silent, reserved nature, tinged with hauteur.

Madame herself held her head with more of stateliness than was her wont, for the republican element, which was beginning to show its head at Saint Lyphar, must be taught to recognize its superiors. Moreover, her heart was sore, for she knew that Gaston, in a day or two, would have to take the field again, fighting under a leader who was famous for reckless bravery and for the desperate chances he took. The name of Jambe d'Argent was, indeed, a menace and a terror to the Blues, and inspired something of awe even in his peasant soldiers. Robert had likewise decided to join the forces of Larochejaquelein and become, like his brother, a soldier of La Vendée. As the noble trio walked along, they were wholly unaware of the villain who lurked in ambush, consumed with envious rage and the fearful passion of greed which caused him to set particular store on the denunciation of Count Gaston, who would bring a high price from the tribunal at Nantes.

"Oh, I shall have the pleasure *de vous pincer,*" he growled, under his teeth, "and you shall squeal, too, for all your titles and honors and your braggadocio airs. And when I have got you, I shall come back again for the other, and for his old hellhound of a father, who threatened to have me beaten from the place. Madame, too, shall have her turn, for all her fine lady airs. The women of the guillotine will soon strip her of all her fine feathers and set her dancing to their tune."

For thus as a storm is often in the air long before it is perceived, neither of the three, as they waved cheerful salutes to the good people of Saint Lyphar, could have guessed that the darkness was already closing around them, and that the doors of a dungeon were yawning for the brave young leader of the Catholic and royal army. Indeed, as Count Gaston walked, he cast significant glances at some of the young men, or made them a gesture which they fully understood, and which referred to those projects which he and Duplessis had debated at the Red Inn, and which had been overheard by Premion's spy.

His mind was full of the glorious enterprise, and he counted over and over the number of men which he should be able to bring to the aid of the intrepid Jambe d'Argent. But he strove to keep up a cheerful and desultory conversation with his mother or with the passers-by, that no suspicion of the truth should dawn upon those who were outside of the secret.

"By this day week," he thought exultingly, "we shall be fighting, and I shall be able to justify Yseult's opinion and to deserve her approving words."

Then a smile passed across his face as he recalled the vision of Yseult at the Red Inn, and his whole heart went out in an impulse of chivalrous devotion to the beautiful girl whom he had loved from boyhood.

"When we have defeated the Blues, as with God's help we shall," he thought, "then, perhaps, there will be our betrothal. Unworthy as I am, she will, perhaps, deign to give me her love and to become my wife."

So idly do men dream, knowing not what the morrow may bring forth, and so darkly may misfortune lower when the sun seems to shine brightest.

Chapter IV

The Arrest of Richard Duplessis

ORIN-PREMION, who had but just recovered from the chastisement which he had received at the hands of Richard Duplessis, was burning with impatience for the return of his spy. He hoped that the man would have but little difficulty in obtaining incriminating evidence against the Vendean. For though it was a maxim of the infamous Carrier, then in the zenith of his power at Nantes, that any individual denounced to the tribunal by a friend of the Republic would be certain of condemnation, still Premion wanted to make assurance doubly sure. Before procuring the warrant, he was, moreover, anxious to have the certainty of Duplessis's presence in the village of Saint Lyphar, for once he had taken to the Bocage or the marshes his capture would be a forlorn hope.

His rage as he waited grew to fever heat. He hated Duplessis. He had always hated him for his personal superiority, his integrity, his fine moral sense, his contempt for meanness. He hated him for the injuries lately received at his hand, and, above all, he hated him as the successful suitor of Jeanne Dumartin. Years before, when Premion had been the son of a swineherd, and himself pursued that calling, he had been smitten with admiration for the girl's fine proportions, her pretty face, her courage, and her industry, and he had dreamed of winning her some day for his wife, as he might have dreamed of winning some great lady, for the daughter of the prosperous innkeeper was at that time far above him, and this had given a spur to his feeling in her regard. He repeated over and over to himself that one day she should be his, and when Jeanne treated him with contempt, for even as a lad he had been crafty and full of meanness, and Jeanne had despised him, he only resolved the more obstinately to overcome her aversion and become her husband.

Now that he could laugh at the idea of her former social superiority, and had himself risen to a higher plane, he was still deeply infatuated with her face and figure. Her personality interested him, her strength and vigor of character, and even her rustic simplicity, had a charm for him such as no fine lady could have exercised, and the fact that she loved another and was, to a certain degree, unattainable, only gave her an added value in his eyes.

Despite his love for Jeanne, he was, however, a man of unusual ambition, and, like many of those who talked the loudest about equality, he had in his heart an unbounded respect for rank and a desire to raise himself to the highest possible level. It had, therefore, occurred to him, as a glorious dream, that he might take to wife Yseult de Breteuil, who was a countess in her own right, and the destined wife of Gaston de la Roche André. She, too, was beautiful. In some moods he told himself that it would be easy to forget Jeanne, and that he would be happier with that lovely lady at his side, the envy and admiration of his associates at the Capital. In these struggles with himself, a powerful argument in favor of Jeanne was his hatred for Richard Duplessis. He could not endure the thought that his mortal enemy should love and be beloved by Jeanne, and he told himself that rather than see her marry Duplessis he would kill her with his own hands, or behold her die upon the guillotine.

In any case, he would put Richard out of his way forever. The course of revolutionary justice was short. It was but a step from the court room to the guillotine.

"He is dangerous to the State, dangerous to my own interests, and my personal enemy," said Morin-Premion to himself, as he paced his room, waiting for the return of his spy. "Those are three very excellent reasons why he should be put out of the way as soon as possible."

As he thus communed with himself he heard the sound of drums, and looking out of the window beheld a detachment of republican troops marching out against the insurgents, and as they went, Premion thought with pride that he had been instrumental in causing their dispatch. He saw the townspeople standing about in groups to look at them. Young men and women, children, and the very beggar who crouched outside the door soliciting alms at the edge of the pavement, all were intent on that brilliant spectacle, and Premion wondered if they coupled his name with the event.

Suddenly he felt his sleeve twitched, and turning, beheld the spy, who had just returned from Saint Lyphar. Premion, forgetting all about the soldiers, sprang eagerly forward with a question on his lips.

"Good news, Citizen!" cried the fellow. "Duplessis is at Saint Lyphar. I saw him talking to a girl at the door of the Red Inn."

A deep flush covered Premion's face, and he scowled ominously. The girl, he thought, must be Jeanne, though it was, in truth, Erminie, for he did not know that Jeanne was then on her way to the Convent of Angers.

"Well?" he said shortly.

"The girl," said the fellow, with a jocularity which Premion felt to be insolent, "was not the one you think."

And he gave a knowing wink.

"It was the sister. That one is far away."

"Far away?" echoed Premion, blankly.

"Yes; gone with the woman de Breteuil from the castle to a convent, where there shall be no love-making."

"To a convent!" cried Premion, a sudden rage seizing him, for he knew that the two girls of whom he had been dreaming were thus, for the time being, out of his reach entirely. "This is some more of that infernal Duplessis's meddling. Oh, he shall pay for it! But you, fellow, have you no better news to tell?"

"I have that in my budget which shall send the Citizen Duplessis to the guillotine when you will, and with him the young Roche André."

The man paused, while Premion's eyes sparkled.

"Go on," he cried, hoarsely, "tell me all."

"And which may, even," continued the wretch, "get the two dainty birds out of their cage, convent though it be."

"Speak!" cried Premion, "and name your own price after."

His face was pale with excitement and full of exultant malice.

"I overheard the conference between the two leaders of the brigands in the parish of Saint Lyphar," began the man.

"And they were?"

"Gaston Roche André and Richard Duplessis."

Premion's breath came in short gasps, as one who had been running.

"What more?" he demanded.

"I saw the Citizeness de Breteuil enter the parlor of the Red Inn, and heard her declare that her heart was with the insurgents. It was with their leader, anyway," the fellow concluded with a grin. "It was plain to see that here were two turtle doves. Only with the aristocrats love is all in fine phrases and bowing and smiling."

"Let that pass," said Premion, bruskly, "and finish your story."

"Jeanne Dumartin was present and talked treason by the yard, and she promised the traitor Duplessis to be his wife at any time he asked for her, and said that she loved him better than anything on earth, and next only to God. She is superstitious, that one; but when she loves a man, she loves him, and isn't afraid to say so, like the pale one from the castle above."

While the spy chattered on, all the light of exultation had gone out of Premion's face, and his pallor was that of the dead. Every word of the wretch's story was as a dagger turning in a festering wound. He knew, then, that he preferred Jeanne to everything, that for her he would renounce ambition, wealth, and all that it could give. Duplessis must first of all be got out of the way. He hated him at that moment with a concentrated fury of hate, such as Satan might have felt toward the first man in his paradise. The scene which the spy had conjured up maddened him. Jeanne, strong, and true, and tender, pledging herself with loving looks and words and smiles to that other, whom he could imagine radiant with happiness, braving death cheerfully for a cause which Jeanne loved.

"We are wasting time," he cried, springing up. "Here is the death warrant, and there is Duplessis waiting to be caged and dragged to the scaffold!"

The spy was half alarmed at the tone and words, spoken in a quick, panting fashion, with a tiger-like eagerness, a fearful ferocity. He stood silently regarding Premion, who turned on him with the question:

"This traitor knows nothing, suspects nothing?"

"No; he was laughing at the wild goose chase upon which you were sending your soldiers."

Ridicule was what Premion could bear least of all, and from him.

"He shall laugh in another fashion before long," he cried out. "He shall die, not all at once, but slowly, lingeringly, and he shall see Jeanne married to me before his eyes by a constitutional priest whom they both despise. Yes; he shall lie chained there, with manacles on his legs and wrists and a weight upon his chest, while the ceremony is in progress."

The spy began to fear that Premion's mind was affected, for even he had never seen conflicting passions so terribly portrayed upon a human countenance. And while he spoke, he fumbled, aimlessly, as one who scarce knew what he was doing, in a corner of his desk. Thence he drew forth a warrant for the arrest of Richard Marie Duplessis on a charge of conspiracy against the State. "To which shall now be added," he cried, with a grim laugh, "a number of other charges."

The curious spy, looking over Premion's shoulder, as the latter bent down to the desk, saw another warrant, marked to be used in an emergency, and bearing the name of Gaston Raoul Marie Albert de la Roche André. The spy stared with all his eyes, for the Roche Andrés were still a power in the district. Premion, angered by his inquisitiveness, and glad to vent the rage which consumed him upon some one, dealt the wretch a cuff upon the ear which caused him to stagger back. For that blow, Premion was one day to pay dearly. At the moment, however, the fellow's look of dark resentment troubled him not at all.

"It was all very well in the old days," grumbled the spy, "when an aristocrat might deal his inferior a blow, but now we are all equal——"

"And I shall make both your ears equal by dealing you a blow upon the other one, if you don't cease your parrot talk. Men are not equal, booby, and never will be. For instance, how could you, with your shock head and villainous face, your ragged clothes and your asinine stupidity, equal me?"

"The aristocrats were right, then?" muttered the man; "and when all is done we shall only have exchanged good masters for bad ones!"

"What are you muttering there?" cried Premion.

The fellow made no answer, and Premion, tying up the documents of which he had need, bade him follow to the office of the National Vengeance.

During all this time, Richard had remained at Saint Lyphar without misgivings of any sort. Premion had never set foot in the village since his departure, and even the stranger who had been seen lurking about for a day or two, and whose presence might have given rise to disquietude, had vanished. Richard was kept busy with his plans for the transporting of the villagers to the farm of Grand Bordage, known as the Camp of the High Meadows. And when he found himself at leisure, he gave himself up not to imaginary terrors concerning Premion, but to tender thoughts of Jeanne, her last farewell, so brave, so womanly, so unselfish.

On the second night after his meeting with Gaston, and his farewell to his betrothed, he was rudely awakened from sleep by the sudden opening of his bedroom door.

The dawn was just rising, faint and beautiful, over Saint Lyphar, with luminous masses of vivid yellow shading into gold. By the dim light Duplessis perceived the figures of three persons, one of whom advanced to his bedside. With a sickening heart, Duplessis recognized his uniform. It was that of the Marat Corps at Nantes, a body of ruffians organized by Carrier for domiciliary visits and the arrest of suspects.

The man, without delay, proceeded to read a warrant for the arrest of Richard Marie Duplessis as a traitor to the Republic.

"You must arise and accompany us at once," said the man, when he had finished reading.

A wild thought of resistance, of possible escape, flashed through Richard's mind. He was strong, courageous, active of body, and resolute of mind, and it seemed to him that he could not tamely submit to such an outrage.

"And what if I do not go with you?" he asked.

The man pointed significantly at his two armed companions standing in the background. Richard's cooler judgment told him that resistance was impossible.

"Who is my accuser?" he asked, as he arose and began to prepare for departure.

"That you will know soon enough."

"I think I might guess even now," Richard said, with a laugh. "There is a hound whom I have lately thrashed. Some dogs, the human sort, are vindictive."

"You had better have a care of your speech, Citizen Duplessis, and so I warn you," said the official.

"Speech or silence will avail little," said Richard, dryly. "But I may strive to con over some pretty phrases which may tickle your ears on the road to Nantes."

The man flushed, seeing that he was being mocked.

"You will be silent enough in the dungeon of the Clock Tower," he said sullenly.

"Oh, indeed," cried Richard, "will there be no such cheerful spirits as yourself there to keep me company?"

"Shut your cursed mouth," roared the man.

"We are not yet at the Clock Tower," Richard reminded him. "But I am now ready to proceed to that delectable abode."

"You'll be there soon enough, brigand, and crying to get out of it," retorted the man savagely.

"Have you inhabited the place yourself—I mean in the good old days before honest men got possession?" Richard blandly inquired, with the same grim humor.

The official furiously ordered his comrades to seize upon Richard, who was in a white heat of rage at having been so easily trapped, and suffered his saturnine humor to play about the head of the Marat man all the way to Nantes. It was a pity that Richard should thus have turned the official's pig-headed indifference into positive hostility, for he was by no means the worst of his tribe, but merely a dull fellow, who had persuaded himself, from certain speeches he had heard and pamphlets he had read, that everything was going wrong with the government, the court, and even the Church, and that he and his comrades were called upon to put everything right by turning the universe upside down. Richard's gibing caused him to regard the young man as an exceedingly dangerous conspirator, who with ready wit and glib speech could deceive all who were brought into contact with him.

"Keep a good watch upon that royalist traitor," he said, audibly, to his companions; "he must be put out of the way of mischief as speedily as possible."

And so saying, he walked on ahead, with dignity, keeping as far as possible out of range of Richard's wit, while he fixed his cocked hat, with its tricolor cockade, securely on his head with the air of a man of determination. All at once Richard's dark face underwent a veritable transformation. He saw Monsieur Gaston, the beloved young Count, advancing toward him. The latter had been at early Mass in the village church, and beheld, with astonishment, Duplessis in the hands of the Marat men.

"My God! Richard, what is this?" he cried, making a few hasty strides toward his friend, whom the captors would have hurried on. Count Gaston bade them stand still by a gesture. Richard saluted the young gentleman with a respect which in no way detracted from the pride and affection which glowed in his face. He replied to the Count's inquiry by a jest.

"It is only, Monsieur le Comte," he said, "that I have a pressing invitation to visit the Clock Tower dungeon from yonder gentleman, who seems to have an intimate acquaintance with the place."

"And who are you that dares to interrupt the members of the Marat Corps in the discharge of their duty?" cried the pompous individual who acted as leader, cocking his hat at the Count in a manner which caused him to resemble an enraged turkey-gobbler.

"I, sir, am Count Gaston de la Roche André," said the young man, speaking with that charm of manner and accent distinctive of his caste; "and may I inquire, in turn, why you have seen fit to arrest my friend, Monsieur Duplessis, in so unceremonious a fashion?"

"Unceremonious!" cried the official, slapping his breast. "I'd have you to know, Citizen Roche André, since that is your name, that there has been ceremony enough."

He was, in truth, a little flustered at being brought into contact with a member of that illustrious house, whose splendor had cast a halo over his youthful dreams. But this only made him fluster the more, especially as his comrades were looking on.

"I, Citizen, am an officer in the Marat Corps, a body of men who have sworn death to all royalists, fanatics, monks, and other enemies of the Republic. I am an official of the National Vengeance Office. I——"

"Enough, sir," said Gaston, with a gleam of humor in his dark eyes. "Any of those titles is sufficient for me."

"And I am supported by two honest *sans-culottes*, members of the same corps," continued the man, in the same pompous tone of declamation.

"All that does not explain why you have seized upon my friend."

"Then, perhaps, this warrant will," the man cried, producing that document, which he held out at arm's length.

The Count, with pale face and quivering lip, saw, indeed, upon it the long familiar name of the playmate of his boyhood, the devoted adherent of his house, Richard Marie Duplessis.

"But with what is he charged?" he asked, desperately, though he knew, indeed, that the particular nature of the accusation mattered little.

"Read, Citizen, read!" said the Marat man, thrusting the paper close to the eyes of the Count.

"Take it away!" cried Gaston, impetuously. "I will not read those unmeaning and long-winded tirades by which you men of the new order swear away the lives of the noblest and the best. It is war of the *canaille* upon all that is sacred."

"Citizen," said the official, growing very red in the face, "you talk like a traitor. I warn you to have a care."

"A care of what?" cried Gaston, scornfully; "of my life, which belongs to our deposed King, God bless him?"

"Amen!" cried Richard, striving to reach his hat, but, realizing that his hands were tied, he let them fall with a melancholy smile.

"I can not wave my hat, Monsieur Gaston," he said, "but you know how I would wave it if I could, crying, 'Long live his Majesty and our beautiful Queen!'"

"I will do it for us both," cried Gaston, snatching off his hat, which he swung into the air with a gesture at once boyish and graceful.

"Long live Louis the Good!" he cried, "and our sovereign lady, the Queen. May God confound their enemies and strengthen their friends!"

The cheer which he raised was joined in heartily by Richard, who observed:

"They have not yet chained my tongue!" And his face reflected the generous glow of youth and loyalty which he saw upon the countenance of his friend.

The cheer which rose and fell, dying away over the marsh lands in rippling cadences, not only aroused the indignation of the Marat men, but their alarm as well. For the village was notoriously in sympathy with the brigands, and should Count Gaston succeed in procuring aid before the prisoner was removed, a rescue would be imminent. And this was precisely the same thought which was occupying Count Gaston's mind.

He had seen Duplessis in the hands of his enemies, and with characteristic impetuosity had rushed toward him alone. Now he regretted from the bottom of his heart that he had not brought with him a sufficient number of his servants and retainers to overpower the ruffians and set Richard free. As it was, he and Richard were both unarmed, the latter being, besides, manacled. Resistance would be futile, and he might only throw away in this vain effort a life which might hereafter be useful even to Richard himself.

"How mad I have been, Richard," he said; and Duplessis, as if divining the outspoken thought, said:

"Better as it is, Monsieur Gaston. Think of the ruin you might have brought on the chateau, on your revered parents, and on another, and all in vain."

"I suppose you are right," said Gaston; "but I can not bear to see you being carried away thus under our very eyes. I will go, too, and, at least, stand side by side with you, and lend you what influence may still be attached to my name."

"No, Monsieur Gaston; no; a thousand times, no!" cried Richard. "You can help me most by making good your escape. Leave Saint Lyphar at once, this very day, and proceed to where you will be in safety."

The official, seeing them exchanging these few words in a low tone, would have separated them, and motioned his companions to force Richard on. But the latter, by a fierce movement, freed himself an instant.

"If you should be in danger," he whispered, "let Jambe d'Argent know of it."

The words were breathed into the ear of the Count, and the face of the latter at once lighted up with intelligence.

"He shall hear of this morning's work," he answered, in the same breathless whisper.

"Do your duty!" cried the leader of the Marat men to his subordinates, and in his anxiety to have his orders obeyed, he laid his hand on the young Count's arm. Gaston shook it off with a gesture full of scorn, and he, who was usually so affable to his inferiors, so simple in his demeanor, emphasized his disgust by delicately wiping his sleeve with a lace handkerchief, which he snatched from his pocket.

"Beware how you lay those polluted hands on a gentleman!" he cried. "I, at least, am not your prisoner."

The subordinates exchanged glances. Richard laughed.

"And now, my men," he said, "do the bidding of your master, who seems anxious to show me his former residence in the dungeon of the Clock Tower."

Bursting with rage, the Marat man marched on, turning to shake his fist after the Count.

"Vile aristocrat," he said; "you are not the first gentleman I have laid hands on, nor you won't be the last. Some of these days I shall drag you, too, away to the dungeons."

He cast looks of spite and rage at his prisoner, whom he would like to have annihilated. For his smiling unconcern as to his own fate and his open contempt of his captors were gall and wormwood to the vanity of a man puffed up by his little brief authority.

"Adieu, Monsieur Gaston!" called out Richard at a turning of the road, casting a last look of love and gratitude toward the young Count, who still stood gazing after him, "Heaven keep you, and if we never meet again, you know what messages I would like to send."

"I know!" cried the Count, "and they shall be faithfully given. But keep up your heart, for we shall meet again, and happily."

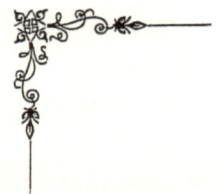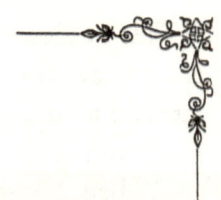

Chapter V

In the Parlor of the Red Inn

THE MEN ASSEMBLED at the Red Inn on the night following the arrest of Richard Duplessis talked in hushed whispers of the events that were taking place in the land, but especially of this latest act of that dreaded tribunal at Nantes. If such an arrest could be made in the very shadow of the chateau, and in the very face of the Marquis and Count Gaston, whom might not Carrier see fit to imprison? Of course, the conversation turned upon the war. Many of those present had already pledged themselves to follow Count Gaston and his lieutenant, and even should these leaders be snatched from them, they were, nevertheless, resolved to take their stand in the ranks of the Catholic and royal army.

"This war has been foretold, my children," said an old man, who was crouching in the chimney corner.

"How is that, Père Michel?" cried a score of voices.

"Why, do you not know?" exclaimed the old man. "My father, may his soul rest in peace, told me often that when the Blessed Father Grignon de Montfort came with his missionaries to preach at Bressuire, a century and a half ago, in the lifetime of my grandfather, God rest him, he stood at the foot of a Calvary, and cried out with a terrible voice."

The old man's voice was low and feeble, and the men, who had been playing cards at the table, dropped them, and those who were smoking took the pipes from their mouth and drew near to listen.

"He cried out," repeated the old man, "'Brethren, one day, God, for the punishment of sinners, shall send into this region a horrible war!'"

Some of the men crossed themselves; others murmured the name of God, of His holy Mother, or of the patron saints of Brittany.

"'Blood shall be shed,'" cried the venerable speaker, raising his voice as he repeated the ominous words of the holy preacher till he, too, seemed like some old-time prophet—"'Blood shall be shed,' so said the saint, 'men shall be slain, the whole country shall be ravaged! These things shall come to pass when my cross is covered with moss.'

"And," said the old man, drawing his hearers together as with a gesture, "the cross of the Blessed Grignon, which stands at Bressuire, is this year entirely covered with moss!"

There was a dead and awful pause. A storm was rising without, the November wind shrieking, as it flew past the inn, like the voices of the dead coming back with fearful warnings, those dead, or those soon to be slain. The bravest of the men shivered, involuntarily drawing closer together with pale faces. It seemed as if in that moment they felt their country's doom upon them.

And in this moment of terror there was a loud knocking at the door. Erminie ran to open it. A man stood without, who hurriedly whispered to her some words. She covered her face with her hands and stood for an instant horror-stricken. Then she entered the inn parlor and announced in a low, trembling voice the arrest of Count Gaston de la Roche André.

The men sprang to their feet with one accord, a storm of execration, of pity, breaking from them. With one voice they cried out:

"How can this be possible? Here, in this very village of Saint Lyphar, with hundreds of true hearts, who would have died for him!"

The messenger, who was none other than Henriot, the valet, now followed Erminie into the room and was besieged by a storm of questions. He was pale, trembling, grief-stricken. He only knew that Gaston had been secretly arrested when on his way to the camp at Grand Bordage and carried off to Nantes. Henriot was too much overcome by emotion to enter into further details, if, indeed, such details were known to him. He was, moreover, hastening on a secret mission, the nature of which he would not disclose, and had only paused to tell the news at the inn and to relight his lantern, which had gone out. The men were left helpless, astounded, panic struck.

"It is time!" cried one. "We must take up arms, and delay not a moment longer."

"Yes," cried the others, "yes; even though our brave leaders are taken from us, we must hasten to the camp of Jambe d'Argent."

"And God's blessing go with you, brave lads!" cried Père Michel, from his station at the hearth. "Oh, that these palsied limbs could march in those glorious ranks! Oh, that this withered arm could strike one blow for God and our King! Wo to me, my children, that it is not so. But my lips can repeat the Rosary, I can hear Mass, I can pray to God unceasingly, for those who fight. Go, my children, go, in the name of God."

"In the name of God!" cried the men, "that is the cry, father. They tell us that the men who followed the brave gentlemen, Larochejaquelein, Lescuri, Bonchamp, d'Elbée, went to battle in God's name with rosary and scapular, and that the hosts of Cathelineau, who is but a peasant like us, and of Stofflet and Charette, stopped in the midst of battle to pray, and set out like Christians from their homes. So shall we, father, so shall we."

It was like a battle cry, and the enthusiasm on the rugged faces of the peasants was as a light from within.

"And we at home, like Père Michel, shall pray for you and ask God to bless your arms," said Erminie, with a sob in her voice.

"Jambe d'Argent shall release our leaders, and lead and give us back our beloved young Count and Duplessis, his lieutenant," said a tall man, who was known as the strongest in the village.

"Yes, yes; Jambe d'Argent shall lead us to victory!" cried the whole assembly. "He is the wonderful leader."

"They say," ventured another timidly, "that he is not a mortal like us, but has come from another world to help the Bretons."

"Oh, it is said," repeated Père Michel, "but we need not credit all we hear, my children. There are some who declare that it is the Duke d'Enghien and the Count d'Artois himself."

"Ah!" cried the peasants, with awe in their voices.

"That may or may not be," said Michel, shaking his reverend head. "God knows that and all things, but it is certain that he is a brave man, and one who can lead. Our own good priests, too, not those from Paris, the new kind, have confidence in him, and that is enough for me."

"Yes; that is enough," agreed the others. "Our curés know what is best."

"Ah, if they had not been taken away from us," lamented Erminie.

"We shall have them back!" cried all the men in chorus.

"Yes, children, we shall have them back," declared Pére Michel. "And now I shall give you my blessing, and you shall go with the morrow's light."

This Michel was regarded as a saint, though he followed the profession of beggar, and sat by the wall of the church with his tin cup outstretched and his dog beside him. His poverty was, to some extent, voluntary, for the Marquis would long ago have provided for him, but in a spirit of penance and through humility, he preferred to beg the trifling alms which sustained him from day to day. His speech was that of an educated man, and it was believed that he had seen better days in the remote district from which he had come.

On the morning following the scene at the inn, when news had arrived of the arrest of Gaston de la Roche André, Michel sat in his customary place, near the wall of the church, with the sunshine streaming all about as a benediction. Presently the Marquis de la

Roche André, with Madame, his wife, appeared at the door of the church. They were proceeding thither to lay their sorrows before the tabernacle. Both were grief-stricken and prematurely aged.

"We must not forget Michel, this morning," said the lady. "Almsgiving touches the heart of God, and the prayer of the poor is all-powerful at the throne of grace."

"Yes, my wife," said the Marquis, "and Michel is truly the servant of God. His rags are greater in God's sight than the purple of the rich."

It was only when the couple stood directly in front of him that the old man raised his eyes:

"Madame la Marquise," said he, "sorrow has touched you, who have healed so many sorrows. It is a divine gift, but heavy for human shoulders."

"You will pray for us and for our dear one," said Madame, in a scarcely audible voice.

"I will pray. I have already prayed. Before the dawn I was in the church, and I told the good God He must give us back our beloved Count Gaston."

The Marquis dropped a liberal alms into the tin cup.

"If you would but let us place you above want!" he said—"you who bring us so many blessings and help us in our sorrows by your prayers."

"But how, then, should I get to heaven?" cried the old man in alarm. "I am too old to work. My health is good. I do not suffer. I must do penance."

"Would that we all did more," cried the Marquis; "this unhappy country might not now be feeling the chastisement of God."

"Yes; that is it, Monsieur le Marquis; the chastisement of God," assented Michel. "For the Blessed Grignon foretold it, and his cross is now covered with moss."

"It is God's hour, and we must submit to His will," said the Marquis.

"But, oh, our hearts are breaking!" said Madame. "Think of my noble young Gaston, my son, my first born."

"Madame," said the old beggar, raising his head suddenly, and pointing with a gesture full of strange solemnity, "that cloud, which has rested darkly upon the chateau, since the early morning, is passing away. Behold!"

The Marquis and his wife turned involuntarily and beheld a dark mass of cloud rolling away southward, and leaving in its stead a flood of golden sunshine which bathed the towers and walls of La Roche André.

"Your son will be restored to you," the old man cried. "I see, I feel it. You have been the protectors and lovers of your people. None were too humble to escape your solicitude. In their miseries they turned to you, in prosperity you rejoiced with them. Therefore, God will watch over your beloved son, and St. Anne and St. Yves, patron of Bretons, will make intercession for him at the throne of God."

"Michel!" cried the lady, "you have brought warmth and comfort to my heart, which was cold and dead within me. God bless you for it, and reward you in His kingdom."

"Amen," said the Marquis, raising his hat reverently. Then, bending his noble head, he added, solemnly: "Your blessing, Père Michel. It will strengthen us in the hour of trial."

To the mobs howling after equality and fraternity in the streets of Paris, it would have been an object lesson in true fraternity and true equality, that of the children of God, to behold this couple, nobly descended and belonging to one of the proudest families of France, humbly bending their heads for the blessing of a beggar, while he, in his turn, with neither rancor nor envy, bestowed upon them that precious gift.

"Because I am old and because I am poor," he said, "God will, in His goodness, hear me, and I ask Him to pour down His blessings upon you both and repay to you a hundredfold all you have done for His poor, and to bless your sons, and to give back to you unharmed him who lies in prison, and that other who has gone to the field."

The Marquis and his wife passed on into the church, deeply moved, and the beggar, left to himself, rejoicing in the warmth of the sun, stroked affectionately the head of his dog, as that animal nestled close to him, and seemed to understand his caressing words. This poor beast was Michel's guide through many a storm, and his protection in the humble hut, at the very outskirts of the village, where he had his abode.

Meanwhile, at Nantes, Morin-Premion paced his apartments, full of a savage joy. He repeated over and over to himself:

"I have them both! Duplessis, how I hate Duplessis!"

He drew in a deep breath, while the force and intensity of that hatred whitened the man's face to livid paleness, and drew his mouth into tense lines.

"And the young cockatoo of nobility," he added, "who has crowed so loud all these years, riding about on his horse through the village streets and tossing pennies to me, the swineherd. Once he struck me a blow. I had got Duplessis down and a friend of mine, a scullion from the castle, was holding him while I pounded. Oh, it was a happy moment, for the fellow had so often beaten me in stand up fights on the village green. But this Count, this Gaston, chancing to pass by, rushed upon me and dragged me up from Duplessis. Once I was up, he struck me a blow which threw me down again, calling me coward and bully. That blow burned and burned, those words rang in my ears, till yesterday, when I saw him brought in a prisoner. His blood shall wipe out the blow and the insult. And as for Duplessis, he shall not die too quickly. My score against him has risen so high. There shall be torture and delay and confinement in the fearful Clock Tower, and I shall go to visit him, and shall talk of Jeanne, yes, of Jeanne!"

He laughed with a malice truly diabolical.

"Oh, I shall be the good Samaritan. I shall speak to him of his sweetheart and tell him to have no fear, for that I, Morin-Premion, will care for her. And then, there will be death at the end of it all, and I shall stand at the foot of the guillotine and see the knife fall and the head be raised and shown to the populace. But what is that?"

He paused and listened. It was the sound of drums in the street.

"I remember," he cried, exultantly, "it is my messenger. He goes into every quarter of the town to announce the arrest of that pestilent royalist, Roche André, and so strike terror into the aristocrats. I wrote out his proclamation for him, and above all I bade him go where the women assemble in the market place, and there beat his drum the loudest and tell his tale. Oh, I have made out this Roche André to be a monster. How the women will grimace when they hear that he set babies up for targets and shot them for practise, while he tied up the mothers near by to watch the sport. They will be ready to tear him into pieces by the time he is brought to trial."

He laughed aloud again, a laugh which sounded hollow and unnatural, echoed through the high ceilinged room.

"Oh, lying, how great is thy power, and how much it has helped the friends of freedom. This Gaston, how it sickened me to hear the women of Saint Lyphar praise him. He wanted the empty bauble of popularity, that was all."

He paced the room, still at the fever heat of his conflicting passions, till the day wore on and the pale sunshine of the November day began to darken. A step was heard upon the stairs outside, and there was a knocking at the door. Premion hastened to open it, saying:

"It is my messenger back. Now I shall hear how the women of Nantes have received my budget of lies!"

The wretch who now appeared had visible signs of agitation about him. His dress was disordered, his red cap awry, his face livid with terror.

"Ho!" cried Premion, "what has happened?" And as he spoke, he regarded the messenger with some anxiety.

"The women!" gasped the youth.

"Well, what of them?"

"At first they heard what I had to tell, and I think at first they might have believed it, but that one in the crowd stood forth and told them I was lying, and that she was from Saint Lyphar, and could prove it."

Premion sprang to his feet with a fearful oath.

"Who was she?" he cried.

"Some said her name was Jeanne."

"Jeanne Dumartin!" cried Premion, swearing again more awfully.

"Was she young? Speak, before I throttle you."

"She was young and old, both," the fellow replied. "Her face seemed young, but she was dressed like an old woman."

"She must be taken at once, at once!" cried Premion, striding up and down the room. "She is in disguise, and has followed Duplessis here. But what did the women do, then?" he asked, pausing abruptly in front of his messenger.

"There was one who supported this Jeanne, and said that she, too, had once known Saint Lyphar, and that the young Count was the friend of the people. Then all the others fell upon me and beat me, and I had hard work to escape with a whole skin. They said lying scoundrels could no longer impose upon the people."

Premion walked up and down in deep and somber meditation.

"I must and will find this Jeanne," he said to himself, "and then a civil marriage at the Mairie will put her forever out of Duplessis's reach."

He seized his hat and coat and rushed out, bidding the messenger await him there. Like a madman he rushed from street to street. For the passion of his life seemed suddenly to concentrate in a glowing heat. His love for Jeanne, if it could be called love, so fierce and terrible was it, and the sweet morsel of revenge which would be his when he could tell Richard Duplessis that Jeanne Dumartin was his wife. These things urged him, as the lash of scorpions. His hate for Count Gaston partook more of the nature of ordinary class hatred; but his hatred for Duplessis burned and boiled up within him like the hidden forces of a volcano. Those who saw him pass fancied that he was crazed, and so he was for the moment by the thought of possible victory near at hand, and of the chance which might not only hinder that triumph, but in some unforeseen manner save Duplessis.

Chapter VI

A Night of Suspense at the Chateau

ENRIOT HAD BEEN despatched on a secret mission, which was to find, if possible, at one of his numerous haunts, the mysterious being known as Jambe d'Argent, and to acquaint him with the arrest of Richard Duplessis and Count Gaston de la Roche André. This faithful valet, who was of that old race which would go through fire and water for the masters whom they served, had had a long and weary journey through the marshes which extend from Saint Hilaire de Rioz to the Isle of Bouin. The dawn was whitening all the landscape when, worn and weary, Henriot came within sight of the chateau. Despite his exhaustion, he still maintained as swift a pace as possible, knowing well the anxious hearts that awaited his coming. He wore, instead of the castle livery, the ordinary peasant costume of brown wool, with a cap upon his head. The castle lay still and cold in the desolation of the morning, which weighs so heavily upon the spirits of the living, when they watch beside the sick or kneel at the bier of the lately departed.

The walls gleamed with an unearthly whiteness, and the windows, like staring eyes, overlooked the dreary landscape. The road leading up to the chateau was both hilly and stony, passing by the great rock whence the castle and the family alike took their name. The family, indeed, had dwelt there since immemorial time, and had taken its share in all the vicissitudes of the nation's history, yet, for the most part, living a calm and patriarchal life. The sons of the various generations had gone successively to fight for king and country on foreign battlefields, or had sat in legislative halls, while the daughters of Roche André, being noted for grace and beauty, had frequently made distinguished marriages. The family had consequently allied itself with some of the proudest houses of France, and its claim was undisputed to a foremost rank among those of the old order, that splendid and brilliant nobility, soon to be no more.

Within the castle it had been a night of agonizing suspense. Consternation sat upon the faces of the servants and retainers. The power of that house, which they had regarded with almost superstitious veneration, and which they had supposed to be as impregnable as royalty itself, had been dealt a fearful blow. Moreover, the young Count himself was sincerely and universally beloved. The old servants who had known him as a handsome and generous boy, the young ones who had grown up with him and been in a sense his companions and playmates, were alike inconsolable. They could not reconcile themselves to the sudden sense of loss, the fear that was in all hearts of being deprived of that beloved presence forever.

The Marquise knelt in her oratory, praying and weeping, or sat beside the Marquis in a silent agony of grief. Her high spirits, the light-hearted gaiety which, preserving the childhood of the heart, had made her so charming a companion for her young sons and their associates and so enlivening a one for her somewhat serious and taciturn husband, had now completely deserted her. It is true that she met misfortune with a calmness and dignity inherent to her nobility of character. She made no noisy demonstration of grief, but strove to control her voice, her features, and her manner in presence of the servants, and to sustain the Marquis, who seemed prematurely old and broken.

As the night wore on, she begged of her husband to take a few hours' rest, but he always replied that rest was impossible until Henriot had returned with news of some kind.

"Your dear companionship, my Adrienne," he said to her, "is more in this fearful crisis than any rest."

"Yes; we have always been a great deal to each other," his wife answered, "and our mutual sympathy tends to support us in this hour of terrible grief."

The look which Madame turned upon her husband while she thus spoke was so full of poignant anguish, so helpless and so appealing, that he turned away his head, unable to bear the sight.

"With the help of Jambe d'Argent," he said, "we may have our loved one back again."

"With the help of Heaven, Albert," said his wife, fervently, and at the same time with something of reproach in her tone, "and through the prayers of our blessed protectors."

"You are right, my dearest, ever right," the Marquis said gently; "but under God this man may come to our aid."

"It is said he has wonderful power and unknown resources," Madame observed, thoughtfully.

"We must not count too much on these peasant tales," said the Marquis.

"But Gaston and Duplessis had confidence in him," cried the Marquise, hastily. "Duplessis bade Gaston have recourse to him in any emergency."

Her voice faltered and broke as she pronounced the beloved name.

"Yes," assented the Marquis, "and it was our boy's intention to have sought his aid for Duplessis. He was actually on his way there, so Henriot reported, when arrested. Duplessis was not one to be deceived, and he and Gaston had actually agreed to serve under him, and were to have brought thither a contingent from Saint Lyphar when the blow fell on them both."

"Some believe this Jambe d'Argent to be a person of noble birth," Madame continued.

It solaced her now to dwell upon these tales which hitherto she had dismissed with somewhat lofty disbelief. If the power and the prestige of this man were what the peasantry believed, then there must be hope for Gaston. It was, in any case, the one ray of light in darkness.

"It might be more probable that he is of obscure birth, but endowed with military genius," dissented the Marquis.

Madame's face fell. She was convinced that a person of obscure birth could do little for her boy. The Marquis, seeing the effect of his words, hastened to add:

"But military genius or genius of any sort is of far more value than name or rank in these evil times. Of the worthlessness of the latter, we are ourselves a sad example."

There was silence between them after that, Madame rising from time to time and pacing the room as one who found inactivity impossible.

"I wonder how soon Henriot can be here?" she said at last. "The faithful fellow will lose no time by the way."

The Marquis looked at his chronometer.

"It is three o'clock now," he remarked.

"Then it will soon be day," Madame said joyfully, "and the day is so hopeful and purposeful. The night shutting one in with the darkness gives a feeling of helplessness."

"I think, my love," said the Marquis, "that if Henriot's news be bad, I shall go to Nantes during the day."

Madame gave a cry.

"You, too, my Albert! O God, no! You must not go. It can not do any good, and will be but thrusting your head into the lion's mouth."

The Marquis had a thought in his mind which he did not care to put into words. He had but lately read of a noble of his own remote kindred who had ridden twenty miles from his ancestral chateau to Paris, and had there managed to substitute himself for his son, condemned to death. When the name was called for execution, the youth lay sleeping, and the father answered to his name and number. The creatures of Fouquier Tinville asked but few questions so long as they were not deprived of a victim. The old man was executed and the son was saved. Could not he do the like, in the last extremity? Aloud he merely said, however:

"If our old name has not lost all its power and influence, I may be able to baffle the schemes of this Premion, and, in any case, my dearest, would it not be better for the head of our house to go and face danger when duty called than to remain here ignobly, and permit the son of that house to perish without protest?"

There was a nobility about the old man, as he spoke calmly and resolutely, which made Madame realize that unless Henriot were the bearer of good tidings, she might have to grieve for this other precious life hanging in the balance. She clasped both hands to her heart, convulsively.

"Am I, then, to be left alone?" she cried.

"Robert will, in any event, be spared to you, I trust," said the Marquis, tenderly.

"Robert! Why, he may be at this moment in presence of the enemy," cried the poor lady. "Besides, think, my Albert, of what the loss of Gaston would be, especially were your precious life likewise imperiled. Think what we two have been to each other. Think of the years, as they have gone over our heads, the joy of spring, the glory of summer, the sad loveliness of autumn, and the long, dark mystery of winter. We have shared the joys and the discomforts of all. We have loved each other, and our love has been as a crown. My mind was yours, our hearts were closely bound, we felt acutely each joy or sorrow in common; we looked on beauty with the same eyes, we admired what was noble and good and true together, and strove to weave it into our lives. We saw each other's faults—yours, my beloved, were scarce perceptible—but to forgive them. Yours was the larger, higher nature, mine strove upward to it. We rejoiced in our children, and in them lived our youth over again, but, nevertheless, we were as one. And now, my Albert, will you shatter the fair mirror of our lives?"

She spoke earnestly, impressively, as if from the borderland of a near parting. She surveyed the whole peaceful panorama of their joint existence at the chateau, and her appeal was so tender, so powerful, that it drew tears from the eyes of her listener. He took her hand and held it.

"Adrienne," he said, "a generation and more has passed since I pledged my love and fidelity to you. You gave yourself to me in your fresh beauty, with all that charm, that wit, and that captivating grace which might have won you a hundred hearts. You were pleased to accept mine, a poor enough gift."

Madame looked at him with that smile which still illumined her face as with a sunbeam. It was more eloquent than words.

"I was not worthy of you, Adrienne," the Marquis went on, "and I had little to offer."

"One of the noblest names in France," said Madame, with a flash of her eyes.

"Be it so," said the old man, with a sad smile; "but I took you from brilliant Paris to live in seclusion here."

"An enchanted solitude!" exclaimed Madame. "O, Albert, how happy we have been."

And at the recollection she broke down utterly and wept. The Marquis soothed her, as though she had been a child.

"Yes; we have been happy, my love," said the Marquis, "but in all that time you have never sought to dissuade me from what seemed my duty. Rather, you have supported and upheld me. Will you fail now?"

Madame raised her tear-stained face and threw back her head proudly.

"No, Albert," she said firmly; "if the necessity arises you shall go. And I shall be, as always, at your side."

The Marquis started.

"My love," he said, "it can not be. You must remain here, where there will be comparative safety for a time at least."

"My security is by your side," she said quietly; "and if we can not save our son, we can, at least, die with him."

"And Robert?"

An expression of anguish crossed the mother's face.

"Robert," she said, "is daily exposing his life for our ruined altars and for the royal cause. If he escape, he will proceed, no doubt, to Coblentz or to England with the other exiles."

"It is true that we have been only discussing a contingency," observed the Marquis, trying to speak cheerily. "Henriot may bring good news, and I may not be needed at Nantes."

"God grant it!" said Madame; "but, remember, whither thou goest, I will go, and if danger threatens one, it shall threaten both."

At that moment the dawn broke, and the light, faint in the first place but gradually growing brighter, streamed into the room, showing each familiar object with distinctness.

"The day is breaking," cried Madame. "I must look if there be any trace of Henriot. It is time he was here, unless he was detained at the camp of Jambe d'Argent, or were stopped on his way."

She pushed over toward the window a powerful glass which stood on a pedestal hard by, and, putting her eyes to it, peered out over the river, as she believed that Henriot might come by boat, and thence to the rocky shore where he was sure to land, and from which the path, steep and stony, led up to the chateau. The Marquis, still seated, turned his gaze in the same direction.

Thus they remained, silently regarding the still morning scene before them, the broad sheet of the Loire, still covered by the haze of the dawn, and the land, faint and misty at first, gradually becoming bolder in outline and more distinctly marked. The water was as yet undisturbed by a single vessel, for even the fishing boats had not yet set forth to break its calmness by the casting of the nets. And as the coldness of the dawn began to give place to the roseate glow of the awakened day, and still Madame saw nothing, she turned from the glass with a faint, weary sigh.

"I see nothing of him," she cried; "can he, too, have been taken? If that were so, all hope is at an end."

"We must go on hoping nevertheless," said the Marquis, "until hope becomes impossible. Think of the difficulties he may have had to overcome, of the caution with which it was necessary to proceed, and of the distance. Then, too, he may have had to follow that mysterious leader from place to place. It is said that he transports himself from one to the other with extraordinary rapidity."

"His help may come too late if he can not be found at once," sighed Madame. "These dreadful tribunals do their work all too quickly, and few has ever escaped Carrier. In this case conviction would be certain, where, as Henriot supposes, that miscreant Premion desires it from motives of private revenge."

They were still talking thus when there was a knock at the door, and on Madame's giving the order to enter, it was thrown open and a servant appeared.

"Madame la Marquise," he announced, bowing, "Henriot is below."

"Send him to us at once!" Madame cried; "but stay, let him have some refreshment first. He must be exhausted."

Then she sank into a chair, nervously folding and unfolding her hands, her self-possession, usually so perfect, utterly deserting her, until at last she sobbed aloud.

"Forgive me," she said to the Marquis, "but this suspense has been cruel."

"Compose yourself, my dearest," said the Marquis. "I hear a step in the corridor."

The Marquis had already resumed his habitual calm and somewhat cold demeanor, and stood waiting for the servant with an impassive countenance. A moment later Henriot entered, saluting first one and then the other with profound respect.

"Speak!" said the Marquis, "my faithful fellow; let us hear without delay the tidings you have brought. But, first, have you taken the refreshment which Madame ordered for you? You stand in great need of it."

"If you, Monsieur le Marquis and Madame, will permit, I should prefer to tell you first all that I have learned."

"Proceed, then," said the Marquis. "Yonder is a chair, for you are exhausted."

"I have seen Jambe d'Argent," said Henriot, still breathless from the steep ascent.

"And he says?" interposed Madame.

"He had already heard of the arrest of Count Gaston and Richard Duplessis, and further discovered that the charges against them were based upon an interview in the parlor of the Red Inn, which was overheard by a spy."

"My God!" murmured Madame.

"In that interview it was made clear that they had not only served in the Catholic army, but were preparing again to take the field."

The Marquis was very pale. He knew the tremendous import of this news.

"Information was lodged at the same time against our young lady, Mlle. de Breteuil."

"How was her name brought into the affair?" cried the startled Marquis. Madame seemed to be utterly incapable of speech.

"She was charged with being in the conspiracy," said Henriot, in a low voice, "because of her presence at the Red Inn on that night."

"Her presence at the Red Inn?" cried the Marquis, in a tone of displeasure, his brow clouding over. "This is an invention of those infamous men, who spare nothing to attain their ends."

"Pardon, Monsieur le Marquis," said Henriot, confused and trembling, "but, perhaps, it is better for you to know that it was true."

The Marquis drew himself up.

"Tell what you know," he said briefly.

"Mademoiselle went there, accompanied by Jeanne and Erminie Dumartin, to bid Monsieur Gaston farewell and tell him of her sympathy with the Catholic army."

"How imprudent!" murmured Madame under her breath, "and yet how natural, how beautiful withal. She sought to encourage my boy by her words and presence."

And the mother's heart felt very soft and forgiving toward this daughter who was to be, who had stepped aside somewhat from the beaten path of ancient tradition in this crisis of her lover's destiny. Not so the Marquis. His brow grew very dark, indeed. Had Yseult been present at that time in the chateau, she would have been made to feel the weight of his displeasure. For ordinarily gentle to a fault and considerate of all about him, he was inexorable in matters of discipline, and exacted a reasonable but unquestioning obedience from every member of his household. He would not, however, discuss the matter with a servant, reserving for Madame's ears his condemnation of the levity and heedlessness, the want of propriety and the needless rushing into danger, which, in his opinion, had characterized Yseult's conduct.

"Monsieur le Marquis," began Henriot, in a faltering voice, "it was all the doing of Jeanne. She reproached Mademoiselle with having no heart, and said she preferred to let Count Gaston go to death without a word of farewell, rather than break a law of etiquette."

"Silence!" said the Marquis. "I can not permit you to transfer this responsibility to any other shoulders. Jeanne was the subordinate."

Madame called the Marquis apart.

"Think of the pleasure she has given to our Gaston by this, which, to my mind, shows a noble heart. To bid him farewell and inspire him by her words to heroic deeds. Is it such a crime? If so, then, I, too, I am afraid, would have been guilty, Albert, in those days long ago. I could not have let you go away, perhaps to death, without seeing you again."

"But it was for him to seek her," said the Marquis, softening, nevertheless, and touched by that allusion to the past days of their courtship.

"He could not and would not for obvious reasons," urged Madame. "It was impossible for him to implicate her, all of us, by a visit to the castle when employed on such a mission."

"She should have had equal prudence."

"She sacrificed only herself."

"Had they been betrothed——"

"After all, what is that but a formality? They love each other, they are destined for each other, and I am certain that Yseult's dignity, with Gaston's chivalrous courtesy, prevented any possible impropriety in the situation."

"You are, after all, my love, but a woman," said the Marquis, "a very charming one and a special pleader. I have already forgiven the fair culprit, and I would it were in my power to ward off from her the consequences of this act, which may be grave enough."

He sighed as he turned again to Henriot.

"Has the little Dumartin been likewise implicated?"

"Yes, Monsieur. Her words were described as treasonable, and her love for Richard Duplessis displeases that scorpion of a Premion, who wants her for himself."

The Marquis shuddered as he recalled a conversation with Duplessis concerning Premion, into which had been introduced the names of both the girls.

"And what further said Jambe d'Argent?"

"That you, Monsieur le Marquis, were to leave the matter in his hands, and that he would do all that human ingenuity could suggest to save the lives of the accused, and to prevent, if possible, the arrest of Mademoiselle and her companion."

"They are still at the convent?" inquired the Marquis.

"Mademoiselle is there, but Jeanne is at Nantes in disguise, hoping for some way of getting Duplessis out of the prison," answered Henriot.

"Imprudence again!" cried the Marquis. "Madness! But I myself will go to Nantes tomorrow."

"Jambe d'Argent expressly forbids it!" cried Henriot. "His words were, 'Let not the old eagle seek to follow the flight of the young. He must remain in the eyrie, or the worst may befall.'"

"Oh, he is right," cried Madame; "it might still further endanger our Gaston and add more victims to the list."

"He bade me assure you," continued Henriot, "that he would move heaven and earth to save these innocent men."

"May God reward him!" exclaimed the Marquise; "he has taken a weight from my heart, for I know, I feel, he will succeed. And now I shall go to the oratory to give God thanks and to pray for His help."

"I will join you there in an instant," said her husband; and when she had withdrawn, he turned again to Henriot.

"You have not told all?" he declared with emphasis.

"The remainder of the message I feared to give in Madame's presence. He bids you be not too sanguine, for that the difficulties are enormous, for that Premion, the villain, will hurry on the execution, if once the prisoners are condemned. 'That beaten hound of a Premion,' were Jambe d'Argent's words, 'will bite hard and will not easily loosen his grip. Still it may be done, and the Marquis need not fear that anything will be neglected. But warn him, again, that he must not come to Nantes. The victims are securely lodged in a fearful dungeon, where he would be thrown, too, altogether powerless.'"

"If I must stay here like a chained animal and permit this horror to happen, God's will be done," said the Marquis. "But when a certain time has elapsed and hope seems to be abandoned and effort at an end, then I will go thither and snatch my boy from the guillotine at the price of my own life."

He spoke rather to himself than to Henriot, of whom he presently inquired:

"What manner of man is this Jambe d'Argent?"

Henriot threw up both his hands, crying enthusiastically: "A most wonderful man, Monsieur la Marquis. He knows everything, even what goes on at the greatest distance. To me, he is not mortal. He has eyes that burn like fire. I found him at the Camp of the High Meadows, but he has many other resorts. I would have feared him had I not known that he was sent down to earth to help the Vendeans."

"God grant him supernatural aid in this case," said the Marquis. "I will see and judge of him myself, please God, at no distant day."

"Not till he gives the signal; he will call you when you are needed," said Henriot. "That was what he said."

The Marquis, pressing into Henriot's hand some gold pieces as a reward of his faithful service, dismissed him to the rest and refreshment he required.

Chapter VII

In the Dungeon of the Clock Tower

RICHARD DUPLESSIS had been confined in that dungeon which was popularly known as that of the Clock Tower, because the victims heard continually the dismal sound of a clock which struck each quarter, thus announcing to the condemned that time was growing short and eternity drawing near. Those confined in this dreary prison were understood to be beyond hope of pardon, and also on the very eve of execution. But the execution was often deferred, thus increasing the torture of the victim by perpetual suspense.

Thus Richard Duplessis lingered, though he had been formally condemned to death, and had heard his sentence with tranquil mien and an undisturbed composure, which infuriated Premion, who stood by with taunts and sneers, drawing only from Richard an expression of the profoundest contempt.

Duplessis had no hope of revisiting his beloved village or seeing Jeanne again. Hope, indeed, as regarded the things of earth, was dead within him, but with cheerful composure he prepared to meet his fate. He lay, heavily manacled, in a noisome cell, crawling with loathsome reptiles, where the swish of the river without filled up the pauses in the striking of the awe-inspiring clock. It was the simple and manly faith of the soldier of La Vendée which kept up his courage in those fearful hours and prevented him from sinking into the abyss of despair. He told himself that he was to give up his life for his beloved country and the faith which he held still dearer, and it mattered not whether on the guillotine or the battlefield. And, if he had to endure the unspeakable horrors of this imprisonment, it was the part of a man and a Christian to resign himself to the inevitable.

Often in his dreams he went back again to the pleasant places of his boyhood, swift runs in the breezy mornings on the Marais with his young companions, merry games of *cache-cache* in the woods of the Bocage, fishing expeditions with his beloved Count Gaston, always his hero and the idol of his boyhood, hours of study at the College at Vannes, whither he had been sent by the favor of the Marquis, and, last of all, his brief courtship and the joy of possessing the love of his noble-hearted Jeanne, who had all the sterling virtues of the Breton woman—a fearless devotion to duty, a self-denial which was almost austere, a beautiful enthusiasm for religion and for country, and all those nobler traits which spring from the life-long practise of the Catholic faith.

Sometimes, even in his waking moments, he strove to bring the past before him, and he recalled, with a half smile and a half sigh, the talk of the lads on the parade ground at Vannes. Their noble aspirations, their determination to die, if necessary, for God and country, their contempt of evil, their generous Utopianism. He seemed to hear Count Gaston talking to the others. He was always a leader in the circle he affected. What boyish earnestness, what inspiration in his fine face, what intense desire to reach out and grasp the finer things of life! And how the others had responded, as the strings of a violin respond to the bow. Well, many of those lads had all too sadly realized their youthful dreams, and had perished in the ranks of the faithful few who surrounded the King, or on the guillotine; others were, like himself, in prison. He was as yet ignorant of the arrest of Count Gaston. But some, on the contrary, had turned aside from the shining path traced out in those youthful dreams, pursuing devious paths. In the ranks of the republican army, in the host of unprincipled demagogues, of whom Premion was a type, at the very revolutionary tribunals were to be found some of those lads who had talked so bravely on the college campus.

He was surprised one morning at the early appearance of his jailer, who brought with him a blacksmith to strike off his manacles. The men would answer no questions, but presently led the prisoner into a well-lighted and cheerful room, which had little save its utter bareness and the grated window to suggest a prison. Here he was better fed and treated with considerable indulgence, being even supplied, at his request, with writing materials.

Thenceforth he spent his spare moments in adding new pages to a manuscript which he hoped might one day reach his betrothed, and into which he poured out every secret of his soul. One morning, shortly after his removal to these better quarters, he was so engrossed with his journal that he did not perceive a jailer, who had entered and was standing observing him.

"My dearest," he wrote, "I wonder if this change to comparative ease and luxury means the approach of death? If so, I shall try to confront it cheerfully and picture to myself that paradise above, where there will be a perpetual feast of all saints, and where we shall surely meet. I wonder how it will be? Shall the faces we were familiar with upon earth be the same in that new brightness? Will the old look we cherished be there, or some other one born of great love and peace? In any case, my Jeanne, it will be there, and there alone, that we shall see each other again. These cruel walls will never relax their hold save to send me to the guillotine."

"That depends somewhat upon yourself," observed the jailer, dryly.

Richard started violently, looking up and, for the first time, perceiving the intruder, who seemed to be peering over his shoulder.

"You have been reading what I was writing!" Duplessis cried, with a swift flush of anger.

"I chanced to see the last sentence you wrote. It doesn't matter. I shall not tell tales," replied the other, imperturbably.

Duplessis, stifling the anger which he knew to be futile, noticed for the first time that this was not the same jailer to whom he had been accustomed, and who had been a particularly brutal as well as taciturn fellow.

"There are ways by which you might open this prison," suggested the newcomer.

"Name them," said Duplessis, looking up quickly.

The jailer came forward and leaned upon the table, so that he was directly confronting the prisoner.

"The surest way," he said, slowly, "would be to sell the Roche Andrés, root and branch, old and young."

"Sell?" repeated Duplessis, not at first realizing his meaning.

"Pretend to have some particular knowledge about them," continued the jailer, coolly, "which will insure their condemnation as enemies of the nation, dangerous to the public welfare."

The man had scarce finished when Duplessis sprang upon him.

"Villain!" he cried, forcing him backward against the wall. "How has your wretched brain imagined such baseness?"

"But your life?" gasped the man, half stifled.

"A thousand lives would not tempt me to hurt one hair of those noble heads," replied Duplessis. "Oh, that any one should have dared to breathe the thought!"

"Softly, or you will kill me," cried the man, for Richard, in his rage, scarce knew what he did—"and it was not by my brain that this plan was laid. Premion——"

Richard relaxed his hold, and the stranger took several gasping breaths to fill his lungs. When he could speak again he began:

"I heard the Citizen Carrier say to Premion that he must and would be rid of those pestilent Roche Andrés, for that, on the one hand, they were forever striving to interfere with the business of the tribunals, and on the other, people were never tired of sounding their praises and encouraging other aristocrats to act similarly. Premion then said that you, who knew so much about them, might be made to turn informer, and that is why you have been brought up from underground and placed in this spacious cell. The same reason has caused the manacles to drop from your legs and arms. It might have been as well for me had they been left on a little longer. But that is by the way."

"Premion dared to say such a thing of me!" cried Richard, who, fairly speechless with rage, had sat through the other's recital with flaming cheeks and eyes aglow with a passion which seemed fairly to scorch the narrator.

"Men measure one another by their own yardstick," the jailer replied, carelessly, and Richard looked sharply into his face, eager to determine whether the man before him was friend or foe to Premion.

"But what was his object?" inquired he. "He does not desire my release."

"Desire it? No," said the man, with a grim smile. "Nor has he any intention of allowing it. He is merely playing a game of fox, with you for the goose."

"Explain yourself!" exclaimed Duplessis, impatiently.

"Before I do so, let me lay before you the advantages of this scheme, leaving Premion, too, aside for the present."

"The advantages of infamy!" cried Duplessis. "I forbid you to say a word, or, prisoner as I am, I fear I shall do you violence."

"As you please," said the other coolly. "I shall, therefore, proceed to the explanation. If once you played his game, Premion would chronicle the same for the benefit of a certain young person, the daughter of a worthy citizen who keeps the Red Inn at Saint Lyphar."

Duplessis made a gesture of displeasure.

"I see you object to the introduction of this young person into the drama, but she has to appear. The tale would not have been a pretty one for her ears, and the Citizen Duplessis would have fallen several degrees in her estimation. Duplessis had sold the people at the castle, to whom he was bound by many early ties. Therefore, Duplessis was unworthy the love of an honest girl, who had not the proper amount of respect for the friends of the nation. Once this design accomplished, Carrier would be made to understand that you yourself were the most dangerous of all suspects, and the guillotine would quickly end your career."

Richard fixed a piercing glance upon the supposed jailer, and asked suddenly:

"Who are you?"

"That will come later. But, as I have said, there are means of escape. I have told you of only one."

"If the others are equally infamous, I warn you again to be silent," said Richard, sternly.

"The other requires wit, address, courage, endurance—qualities which I believe you possess," said the other. "With them you may outwit Premion and the devil himself. Once out of prison, you may put these same qualities at the service of Count Gaston de la Roche André."

The man's manner was that of one who had suddenly thrown aside a mask, and Richard stared at him in astonishment. He perceived, too, for the first time, that he was attired rather as the servant of some great family than as a turnkey in the Revolutionary prison.

"How do you come here, and in such a dress?" demanded Richard.

"Oh, I am the valet of a nobleman, imprisoned here at first, but having been converted to Jacobinism and promising to reveal family secrets, I have been assigned to duty as a jailer, and I wear my livery as a sign to proclaim my conversion."

"You have done this thing!" cried Richard, looking at him with loathing. "You can coolly tell me that to save your own skin you have betrayed the family whom you served?"

"Well, as the family to which I am supposed to belong is non-existent, the mischief is not great," said the other, calmly. "I am to give testimony as to the vices of the nobility at a notable trial which comes off next week."

"You will do so?" inquired Richard.

"By that time I may have gone, say to the seashore for my health," laughed the man. "Perchance, if all goes well, you may bear me company, and the young Count, too."

"You have twice spoken of Count Gaston," Richard observed, "as though he were in danger."

"Well, he does run some risk in being the guest of the nation in one of these delectable abodes," replied the stranger.

"Count Gaston in prison!" cried Richard, sinking into the chair from which he had risen. "Gracious heaven!"

He covered his face with his hands and groaned aloud. His own misfortunes had never drawn from him such a manifestation of feeling.

"If you would save him, you must put by all weakness," commanded the unknown. "Rouse yourself. We shall work together."

"You are, then, a friend?" Richard asked.

"I am, and had you listened to my first proposal the guillotine might have had you, and welcome."

"Who are you, then?" asked Richard for the second time.

"You may, perchance, have heard of Jambe d'Argent?" said the man, and he pointed significantly to a small, circular band of silver which he wore about his leg, covering a spot where he had once received an injury.

Richard knew that it was from this circumstance that that remarkable man had derived his name. A light broke over the prisoner's face as he cried, with a glow of enthusiasm:

"Is it possible that you can be that great leader himself?"

Jambe d'Argent nodded, a rare smile breaking the darkness of his face.

"And yet," added Richard, sorrowfully, "I thought Jambe d'Argent knew something of me, and that he never would have dreamed of trying me by an infamous proposal."

"Listen, Duplessis," said the other earnestly. "I knew you, I believed in you, I trusted you, though we have never met, else I had not been here. You have done work for me, and done it well. You were about at the time of your arrest to act as one of my most trusted lieutenants, but these are evil times, and the sufferings you have undergone might well have tried a weaker soul beyond endurance. Only the finest metals come forth from such a fire. Therefore, forgive me, for, though I had scarce a doubt of how you would pass through the ordeal, it was, nevertheless, a happy though a perilous moment for me when you pinned me to the wall yonder."

The humorous smile which played over his fine face as he spoke was touched with tenderness. "God helping us, you shall be saved, and the heroic young Gaston de la Roche André, too."

"Of what is he accused?" Richard asked, mournfully.

"Oh, the usual counts of the indictment, an aristocrat, an enemy of the people, with many slanderous inventions added, and, last of all, the specific charge of treasonable conspiracy. His conference with you in the parlor of the Red Inn was overheard by a concealed spy of Premion."

Richard groaned again.

"Then he is lost!" he cried.

"Unless we can save him," suggested the other.

"Unless *you* can do so," answered Richard. "Of what use am I?"

"Few things are impossible to the strong and brave and true," said the pretended jailer, and Richard, looking at him with admiration, exclaimed:

"It is incredible that you should be Jambe d'Argent, that renowned captain of whom such marvelous things are told!"

"Times like these make ordinary men into heroes, and heroes into demi-gods," said Jambe d'Argent, with his inscrutable smile.

He was a tall man, finely proportioned, with a noble, expressive countenance, changing at every thought, with a smile now playing about the mobile lips or the stress of grief darkening the steel-blue eyes. As to his dress, he was seen under aspects so protean that it could never be adequately described.

"I must go now,' he said, addressing Richard. "But if you are this night removed to the prison hospital, do not be surprised."

"To the hospital!" cried Richard, in amazement.

"You are a very sick man, Richard Duplessis," continued Jambe d'Argent. "You are ill of a fever, and do not know anything that is passing. Your mind is disordered, and whatever you say is to be set down to the wanderings of frenzy."

Richard, beginning to understand, laughed outright.

"So I have anticipated any possible imprudence on your part," declared Jambe d'Argent.

"You have left me no loop-hole at all, monsieur," Richard said; "but I think I shall keep dumb."

"It may be as well, though you may, if you wish, mutter strangely, Richard, and speak in disjointed phrases. And now, adieu, or, rather, *au revoir*."

"Shall I see you again, then?" asked Richard, eagerly. He already felt for this stranger an unusual attraction, that glamor which this mysterious leader exercised over so many.

"Of course; I shall see you at midnight. You have to be taken to the infirmary. My republican zeal will be anxious to save the life of so valuable a witness for the State. I shall heap attentions upon you, and, if I should chance to kill you with kindness, I shall have you buried as speedily and as privately as possible to avoid the anger of one Premion."

He said these words with special significance. Then, as he opened the door and passed out, he put his finger to his lips to insure secrecy. And Richard found himself once more securely locked in, but with a heart how much lighter it is easy to imagine. Even the remote prospect of escape, the rare chance of regaining his liberty, was exhilarating to Richard's healthful and buoyant nature.

The bell of the Clock Tower had just tolled out midnight, the hour of mystery, by excellence, the ghost-haunted hour, the hour which thrills one with vague apprehension, the hour of crime, the hour when the dead today parts from the living tomorrow. The door of Richard's cell creaked on its hinges, admitting Jambe d'Argent, with two other men.

"This is the patient, Citizen Doctor," said the first named. "I would like you to examine him, for his condition appears to me serious, and were he to die the nation would lose an important witness, and the Citizen Premion would be sorely disappointed."

The cell was very dark, only the light of the lantern which one of the men carried illumining it. This light was turned upon the pallet bed in the corner, but Richard was not there. He was discovered sitting at the table, his head resting on his arms.

The doctor bent over him, inquiring how he felt, but, receiving no answer, he felt his pulse, passed his hand over his forehead.

"The man is in a raging fever," he pronounced, "and must be removed to the hospital without delay."

"That is as I thought," said the pretended jailer, "but I wanted your authority in support of mine."

"Seize him, then, by force, if necessary," ordered Jambe d'Argent, and the burly fellow, who stood in the background, sporting his *bonnet-rouge* ostentatiously and odorous of stale tobacco, came forward to execute the order.

"We must carry him to the hospital," went on Jambe d'Argent, speaking in a loud, swaggering tone. "I will lend a hand, and he must have every care, for his life can not be spared yet till he has brought those cursed aristocrats of Roche Andrés to the national razor."

The man addressed laughed thickly and coarsely, saying:

"Never fear, citizen, we will take care of him," and shaking Richard by the shoulder he cried in his ear: "Wake up, my cockatoo, and come with us. You shall have a good *sans-culotte* or two to wait upon you."

Richard muttered a few broken words, but made no attempt to rise, and the supposed jailer gave command.

"Raise him and we will carry him between us."

The other obeyed, and with some slight resistance on the part of Richard, who seemed to be in a stupor, he was borne to the prison infirmary and laid upon a bed. One or two other patients were in the room, and to the bedside of these repaired the doctor, holding no further converse at the moment with Richard. The ex-valet went from bed to bed, devoting particular attention, however, to Richard, binding a thick bandage about his head and offering him a cooling drink. Those in the room took little heed of what went forward. The man in the adjoining bed seemed overcome with the double weight of his imprisonment and his sufferings, and the other inmate of the room conversed so earnestly with the doctor that Richard and his attendant were left practically unheeded.

"You must drink this cup," the ex-valet said, in a quick, decided whisper, "but not till the hour of three has struck from the great clock in the tower. Then swallow its contents to the dregs."

"And what will follow?"

"Ask no questions! Leave that to me!"

There was a passing gleam of distrust in Richard's mind. This man, indeed, represented himself as Jambe d'Argent, but how was he to be sure? He met the eyes of the ex-valet fixed upon him. They seemed to read his thoughts.

"Your distrust is misplaced," he said, in the same hurried whisper, "and the alternative of trusting me is the guillotine for yourself and your friends. For know that not only Count Gaston, but Mademoiselle, too, is accused of conspiracy, because of her presence at the Red Inn, and will soon be arrested. The name of Jeanne Dumartin also figures on the list of the accused, and would be taken, even had she not left the shelter of the convent to come here to Nantes in an effort to save your life."

"Merciful God!" cried Richard. Then he added firmly: "Have no fear, I will drink the cup."

"The potion must be taken at three o'clock," cried the ex-valet, raising his voice, so as to make himself heard by all. "Doctor, this stupid fellow can not be made to understand."

The doctor approached, and succeeded at last in fixing Richard's attention.

"It is often the case with fever patients," he said; "they listen to an authoritative voice."

He turned to the man in the next bed.

"Should he appear unconscious, force him to take the draft," he said.

The man promised.

"Even if you have to force it down his throat," continued the doctor.

"He shall take it," promised the man.

The doctor and the ex-valet then withdrew, and Richard, left alone, mused upon his strange surroundings, and the things that had befallen, fearing to sleep and awaiting always the tolling of three o'clock. He suspected that the doctor was in the secret, and felt a warm glow of gratitude to Jambe d'Argent, who had thus endangered his own life and liberty in so desperate an attempt. As the booming, ill-omened sound of the Clock Tower bell rang out three, and before Richard had time to move, the man in the next bed cried out to him:

"Here you, Citizen, drink your potion. It is to make you well for your business, which is to slit the throats of fat aristocrats. Up with you, and take it!"

Richard, affecting to be rudely awakened from slumber, raised himself upon his elbow, and, after a moment or two of apparent bewilderment, obeyed the reiterated order of his neighbor, and drained the cup to the very bottom, having first commended his soul to God.

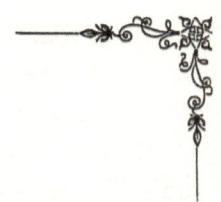

Chapter VIII

Trial of Count Gaston de la Roche André

O N THE DAY following Richard's removal from the prison cell to the hospital, Count Gaston de la Roche André was summoned before the Revolutionary tribunal on a variety of charges, of which the chief was his conference at the Red Inn of Saint Lyphar, with other traitors, in which was clearly stated his intention of taking the field in the army of the brigands, and heading the men of his own village in an attack upon the Blues. Premion did not directly appear as the young man's accuser, leaving that to the spy who had overheard the conversation. But he took his place among the motley crew which sat in judgment at the bar of Carrier, presided over by that notorious ruffian himself.

The room was crowded with men and women all hostile to the accused, and anxious to contribute, by their applause, at least, and their hostile demonstrations against the prisoner to his condemnation. The name was called:

"Gaston Albert Charles Marie de la Roche André, *ci-devant* Count and officer in the Royal Regiment."

There was a pause in the crowded court. The name had been long a power in that region. Many in the multitude had received benefits from the family, or had trembled at the strong arm which the Marquis had occasionally put forth against evildoers. The door being opened, there entered a young man of slender and graceful build, whose nobility of aspect for a moment overawed the fierce gathering. His arm was grasped by the same furious Jacobin who had gone to Saint Lyphar on a spying expedition and returned with a full budget of information. He was in the pay of Premion, but he had served Carrier well before now by denouncing numberless priests and aristocrats to the tribunal. His dark face, surmounted by the liberty cap of flaming red, was aglow with the eagerness he felt to secure the young man's condemnation.

For he had once been in the employ of the Marquis de la Roche André, had been convicted of theft and pardoned by the clemency of his employer, who had, moreover, obtained for him employment at a distance, and had supported his mother and sisters in his absence. The Marquis had failed to recognize him upon the occasion of his visit to Saint Lyphar, but the fellow's wrath had flamed up bitterly against him, especially when the old gentleman had threatened to have him beaten from the place. He was, in fact, one of the most blatant of all the *sans-culottes* who indulged in fiery tirades against the aristocrats who cumbered the earth, oppressing the poor and deserving, and trampling on the liberty of the nation.

"Your name?" demanded the President of the tribunal.

"Gaston de la Roche André."

"Your station?"

"Count and eldest son of the Marquis de la Roche André."

"Your occupation?"

"Till recently an officer in the Royal Regiment."

"Note, citizens, worthy republicans, that he acknowledges having borne arms against the people."

"Having borne arms in the service of the King and against the enemies of France!" corrected Gaston.

"King? There is no King in France."

"I refer to his late Majesty, King Louis the Good," answered Gaston, a flash of enthusiasm lighting up his face.

There was a howl from the more advanced republicans. Gaston looked around him with disdain.

"The King was a tyrant and a traitor," cried the mob. "So are the aristocrats. Down with all tyrants! Death was too good for Capet and the infamous Austrian woman, who hated the French."

Gaston's eyes flashed.

"I trust they are both in heaven!" he said, solemnly, raising his voice so as to be heard through the room.

"Or in hell, where you will go to join them soon!" said the angry chorus.

Gaston smiled contemptuously, but made no further remark. His silence seemed still further to aggravate the yelling crowd.

"Silence!" roared the President, "and let us hear the crimes of which this prisoner has been guilty."

"Yes; let us hear!" cried the mob.

"'First, he was an officer in the detested Royal Regiment, and took part in that infamous orgy at Versailles, being observed to join in that traitorous anthem known as *Richard, O mon Roi*," after which he received a cockade from the Austrian.'"

A howl of rage and derision sounded through the court and out of the window, echoing through the streets of the once sober, commercial town.

"'Second,'" continued the President, "'he has been since in correspondence with *émigrés* and foreign traitors.

"'Third, he is himself a notorious oppressor of the people, being known to enforce his commands to an inferior by a blow.'"

"Blow, indeed! He shall get blows enough, if we can only get at him," shrieked a fury from amid a group of women.

"'Fourth, he has deprived his dependents of the necessaries of life in order to spend money in Paris and Versailles.

"'Fifth, he has been detected in endeavoring to poison a well in the neighborhood of his own chateau.'"

"Burn him! Choke him! Tear him to pieces!" roared the human monsters standing by.

"'Sixth, he has aided the old aristocrat, his father, who shall presently be brought to justice, to enforce the levying of the *corvée*, the tithes, and other taxes vexatious to the people.'"

"Down with the *corvée*; we shall mend their roads no more, these vile aristocrats. We shall make them mend ours, if they are not all killed by the nation!" screamed the chorus.

"'Seventh, he has been known to set up innocent babes as targets for his archery.'"

A roar of execration followed this announcement. The President, again commanding silence, proceeded to give a list of other charges too infamous for repetition.

Gaston had been listening indifferently to the first counts of the indictment, which were the ordinary ones against aristocrats, and had only manifested emotion once, when the name of his father was mentioned, accompanied by a threat. Now, however, a growing expression of wonder, of horror, of incredulity, overspread his face as he listened to the latest charges. They were followed by a wild tumult, the women, in particular, striving to get near him, and, as they said, rend him where he stood.

"The monster! The shameless villain! The accursed aristocrat! Burn him! Flay him! and smoke out the nest he comes from!"

There was a flush of shame upon the young man's face that such things should be said of him here, in the open court, infamous slanders which none dared question.

"I deny every word of those final charges!" the prisoner cried at last, unable to bear it longer. "They are false and slanderous, manufactured merely to procure my condemnation, which can be obtained without them. It is sufficient to be an officer of the King and a gentleman to suffer death in these days. Therefore, why vilify me?"

His voice rang out clear and commanding, and it was followed by that of a woman.

"He tells the truth; the Count is noble and good. These charges are base lies, every one of them."

The Count fancied there was something familiar in the tone, and turned his gaze toward a part of the room where stood the figure of a girl. She raised her hand, with a tiny scroll in it, as if to attract his attention. But he instantly averted his eyes, for it occurred to him that the slightest evidence of collusion with her might insure her destruction. Despite her disguise, he knew her instantly, and, unfortunately for herself, so did Premion. Her voice had sent a thrill through him, and he knew that in her courage, her loyalty, her very defiance of himself, he loved her as he had never done before. Moreover, here was the hour of her triumph. He knew that she would be present at the trial of Yseult, which was to follow that of Gaston, should Carrier's messengers bring her thither in time, having ventured all to be near her friend in the dread ordeal.

He gave a hasty order to one of his subordinates to seize her and bear her quietly away to the prison for women, which was in a former convent. As the man took her by the arm, ordering her to follow him, Jeanne resisted, and Premion, stealing up behind her, whispered:

"Go quietly. You were mad to come here. A warrant is out for your arrest, but I am your friend, and can save you."

Jeanne cast one look of unutterable loathing at him, and, raising her voice, appealed directly to the court.

"This man Premion!" she cried, boldly, "has tried to bribe me to deceive the tribunal. Though knowing that I am a suspect, he has offered to have me conveyed privately away. Therefore, I denounce him as a plotter against the people!"

There was a murmur in the court.

"For myself," went on the brave girl, "I demand, if I am to be tried, a fair trial before the court. I demand to be taken to the ordinary prison."

"She speaks well," cried several. "She shall not go to prison. She is a good woman and a friend of the people. She has lived among us, and we know her. *À bas* Premion!"

"Yes; *à bas* Premion!" cried Jeanne, "who makes money by delivering up innocent people, and spends it at the capital."

Premion withdrew, deadly pale, into a corner. He saw that he had overreached himself, and he felt that Carrier's eye was upon him.

"I wanted to save the woman because of old acquaintance," he stammered. "I knew she was not a traitor."

"The Republic acknowledges no old acquaintance," said Carrier, severely. But it did not suit him to press matters against a confederate.

"As for you, *Citoyenne*," he said, addressing Jeanne, "you shall have your wish. We shall not trouble ourselves to take you to prison. You are found guilty of treasonable words, of contempt of court, of abetting aristocrats. You shall die tomorrow at four with this execrable Roche André."

Premion narrowly repressed a cry of agony, while Count Gaston, shaking himself loose from the grasp of his accuser, sprang forward.

"I protest," he cried, "in the name of justice, in the name of the nation. You shall not harm this helpless woman, a daughter of the people like yourselves, who has but proclaimed her loyalty to the family which has befriended her. Women of France, I appeal to you. She is innocent, wholly innocent."

His voice was vibrant and passionate with that rare quality which goes to the heart.

"He is right," said some of the women. "The girl has spoken foolishly, but she has done no harm."

Others cried out vehemently to let the aristocrats and their friends perish together.

"Men, citizens, will you permit this atrocity?" cried Gaston again. "I have listened to charges against myself which have caused me to flush with shame. But I am ready to meet death as a brave man should, and to show you upon the scaffold how a gentleman dies.

You shall not be balked of your revenge. I admit love and loyalty to the late monarch. I am proud to have served in the Royal Regiment, and to have been present at that banquet at Versailles, a last expression of devotion to our hapless sovereigns. But I implore you to spare this woman, and I will make no defense. I will die without protest."

His words produced an effect upon some, and Premion ventured to applaud them. He was silenced by a threatening glance from the President, who, with cold brutality, proceeded:

"Citizen Roche André, we have heard you, lying after the manner of your kind, but you have forgotten to add to your list of indictments that which properly stands at the head. You have said nothing of your conference at the Red Inn of Saint Lyphar with the arch-traitor, Duplessis, by which you pledged yourself to bring a force of brigands to the camp at Grand Bordage. That story has yet to be told. Witness, stand forward!"

Gaston could not repress a start. The news was most unwelcome to him, for, although he knew that he would be condemned in any event, he feared that this new evidence might serve to implicate others, and to bring even his beloved father and mother into danger. The spy, who had overheard all that happened, now proceeded to give a minute but highly colored account of the interview between the two leaders, and, pointing abruptly at Jeanne, he said:

"You were right in arresting this traitress. She, too, was there with another, and encouraged the brigands by every means in her power."

"She shall die!" said Carrier, sententiously. "She shall change the little pleasure excursion I had planned for her to a drive in the national omnibus."

So he facetiously called the tumbril.

"You, Citizen Roche André, shall go to the guillotine tomorrow at four, and the woman Dumartin shall accompany you. I like to unite those who love each other."

"Shame, you hound!" cried Gaston, while even Premion clenched his fists convulsively in his corner. And at this moment an unexpected thing happened. A woman in a mobcap, and wearing the ordinary dress of the people, stepped forward.

"If you are to die, Gaston, for no other crime than that of being a true and loyal gentleman," she cried, "my place is at your side. I am equally as guilty as Jeanne. She shall not die alone. For me and for those I love she has come here. At least, I will go with her to execution."

For the first time Count Gaston turned deadly pale and showed signs of deep emotion.

"My God!" he murmured. "Holy Mother of the Redeemer, you alone can save her!"

"And so the ball rolls!" cried the President, chuckling at his own wit. "We shall soon have every woman in the room anxious to die with this fascinating aristocrat. But who are you? Your name?"

"Yseult de Breteuil."

Carrier gave a long whistle.

"I have just sent my men to the Convent of Angers in search of you. So, they thought you were safe with the holy nuns, ho, ho! instead of at Nantes, where the pretty Count was to be seen."

"Cease your intolerable brutality," cried Gaston, "and go on with the trial!"

"Oh, my popinjay, I'll go on fast enough," he said, "and you'll have this pretty bit of womankind with you tomorrow afternoon on your driving party. Don't be afraid."

He then turned to Yseult.

"Your condition?" he asked, roughly.

"Countess de Breteuil."

"Your relation to this man?"

Yseult hesitated. For the first time it flashed upon her that she had placed herself in a false position.

"I have the honor to claim her as my betrothed wife," interposed Gaston, "though the formal ceremony has not yet taken place."

Yseult flashed a quick glance of gratitude toward her chivalrous young lover.

"Is it as he says?" inquired Carrier.

Yseult bent her head.

"Then," said the wretch, with his cold, malicious sneer, "as there is no marriage in the heaven of the aristocrats, I shall have to send you both to hell to celebrate your wedding. We have plenty of evidence against you, Mistress. Your treasonable talk and conspiracy with traitors at the Red Inn of Saint Lyphar are before us in writing. Witness, identify this woman."

The *sans-culotte*, who had already figured so largely in the trial, eagerly obeyed. He swore without doubt that Yseult had been present at the inn, and had urged on the brigands to kill all the Blues.

There were pity and admiration on the faces of many. But none dared speak. The fate of Jeanne had awed them.

"Can we not find a husband for the Dumartin woman?" asked Carrier, with the coarse humor habitual to him, "that we should have a quartet. I am fond of weddings myself."

His cold eyes rested on Premion, who cowered. But it passed over him again. Premion was useful.

"Citizen," said the accuser of Count Gaston and the two girls, "I have knowledge that the woman before you has promised to marry the notorious traitor, Duplessis."

"Capital!" cried Carrier. "Bring him here without delay. Is he at Nantes?"

"In the prison of the Clock Tower."

Carrier referred to his notes. "He is, then, the arch enemy of the people, Richard Duplessis?"

"The same."

"Cause him to be brought hither. They shall all dance to the same tune."

A messenger was despatched, and deep silence fell upon the waiting court. Count Gaston exchanged with Yseult glances which conveyed far more to her than the most eloquent protests of affection, and he contrived at last to draw near where she stood, with her hand resting upon Jeanne's shoulder.

"You have done me infinite honor, Mademoiselle," he whispered.

"There was no choice," Yseult said, with her eyes upon the floor.

"Had there been, would you have had things otherwise?"

Yseult hesitated a moment, then she answered:

"At such a moment concealments are idle. No, Gaston; I would not have it otherwise."

"Let me offer you now, in this terrible scene, my full and entire devotion, the love of a whole life. I am yours in death, as I would have been in life."

"And I pledge myself likewise to you," cried Yseult. "O, Gaston, we love each other, and that is the only brightness in the gloom."

"Courage, my dearest. Death, after all, is but a step to life."

"It will be easy, since we die together," answered Yseult.

"Silence, there!" roared Carrier, who had perceived the two whispering. "Separate the prisoners."

But those few words had been enough. Each felt that they lifted a weight from the other's heart. Gaston had been anxious to seize the first possible moment to declare his love for Yseult, feeling that she had been placed in a difficult position by the announcement of a betrothal which had never really taken place, and which presupposed that declaration on his part had not as yet been put into words.

And he heard the avowal of love from her lips with a feeling of intense joy and thankfulness. He had always loved her with the tender, chivalrous love of his fine nature, and had dreamed of her as his wife, while from boyhood upward he had admired her with a passionate admiration as the type of all that is beautiful and lovable in womanhood. Yseult, on the other hand, though she had long known of Gaston's sentiments toward her, had rejoiced at the force and sincerity which he had put into the few words it had been possible in such surroundings to speak. They were betrothed now; in the eyes of heaven, at least, no formal ceremony could make them more to each other, and she was glad in the consciousness that, had their marriage ever taken place, it would not have been one of those merely conventional unions so common in France. It was curious how this feeling of gladness predominated over those other emotions of fear, of horror, of dreadful expectancy.

Presently the messenger returned from the prison.

"Where is the prisoner?" demanded Carrier, impatiently.

"He can not attend the tribunal."

"For what reason?"

"He died this morning at three o'clock."

Now, even when deaths were of an hourly occurrence, there was an impressiveness about this announcement which struck all present.

"Where is the Citizen Landriot, his jailer, late valet to an aristocrat?"

"Gone to superintend the burial."

"Can he not be found? I wish to speak with him here."

"I will find him, if possible, Citizen."

There was, meanwhile, a bustle and stir among the prisoners. Jeanne had fainted. Count Gaston and Yseult bent over her, murmuring exclamations of horror at the news. Premion gave vent to a fearful oath. Duplessis had, then, escaped his vengeance. Jeanne, by plentiful applications of cold water, was brought to herself. Premion drew near as she came to herself, and with pale face and eyes ablaze scornfully regarded him:

"You, you are his murderer!" she cried.

Premion made a deprecatory gesture.

"It is the more to be regretted," he said blandly, "since the Citizen Duplessis had offered to give testimony which would implicate the Marquis de la Roche André, his wife, and younger son."

"It is false!" cried Jeanne.

"You base cur!" exclaimed the Count, furiously. "Can you respect nothing, not even the dead?"

"I have here a memorandum signed by himself," declared Premion, "which you are free to examine."

"I will look at nothing, hear nothing, against this man who was my friend," cried Gaston, vehemently. "I knew him to be loyal alike to faith and friends and country."

Jeanne cast upon him a look full of gratitude.

"It matters not, since the fellow is dead," interposed Carrier. "He would have sold these aristocrats today, they him tomorrow, if the chance offered, and what would it matter to honest republicans? I must cause a searching inquiry into the manner of his death, and, perhaps, I may send this precious ex-valet, who had the charge of him, to make up Madame Guillotine's quartet. He should not have let him die."

But as the ex-jailer could not be found, the court was declared adjourned, and the prisoners were ordered to be conveyed back to the dungeon of the condemned, under the ominous clock.

Henriot, who had been despatched to Nantes, hastened home with the fearful tidings. He contrived to see the Marquis first, that he might acquaint him with all that had occurred. The Marquis received it with the composure and dignity of a gentleman and a true Christian. But it was a sore task to repeat that awful news to his wife, the more so that he now regretted he had not sooner gone to Nantes and made an effort, at least, to save his son. He had been prevented from so doing by the counsels of that mysterious man, who had failed completely in his promises.

The Marquis found his wife seated, with a copy of the "Imitation" in her hands, near the latticed window of her chamber.

"My dearest," he said, seating himself beside her, "you have your thoughts fixed even now on the ultimate destiny of all Christians."

"Yes, Albert," she answered, "my heart is sad and heavy with premonitions of coming evil, and I am reading here those royal maxims of faith, which, alas! are so far above me."

"What verse were you reading?" inquired the Marquis.

Madame read aloud:

"'Thou shouldst rather rejoice and give thanks, yea, account this as a special subject of joy, that, afflicting thee with sorrows, I do not spare thee!'

"That is a hard saying, Albert," she commented.

The Marquis spoke very gently.

"Can you rejoice and give thanks that, afflicting, He does not spare thee?" he asked.

"My God, my husband!" cried Madame, "what would you say? What tidings have you to communicate?"

"Have patience, have courage, my beloved Adrienne. News has reached me from Nantes. Gaston is condemned to die."

The mother covered her face with her hands, giving utterance to a cry of anguish so piercing that, though not loud, it rang out upon the air, startling a mother bird which was feeding its young in a nest near the window.

"There is nothing wanting of nobility, generosity, piety, courage," went on the Marquis. "He will die as a true son of France and of the Church."

"Oh, my first-born, my well beloved," wailed the mother, in a grief that seemed for the moment impervious to consolation, and which seemed to isolate her even from her husband.

"And he will not die alone!" continued the Marquis.

The mother waited, asking no question.

"Yseult de Breteuil is with him!"

Madame, startled out of her lethargy, repeated:

"Yseult?"

"I will tell you the whole sad story," resumed the Marquis, "and how that humble heroine may be said to have given her life in trying to save our boy by creating a diversion in his favor."

Madame listened with drooping head while her husband related to her every detail of that strange scene in the court-room, as it was reported by Henriot, so full of poetry and romance, of chivalry and self-devotion, on the one hand, so overladen with horror and foulness and black iniquity, on the other. When the narrative was at an end, husband and wife sat together silently awhile, striving each for the other's sake to master the sorrow which consumed them both. Then the Marquis, taking the book from his wife's hand, turned to the forty-eighth chapter, and read aloud, in a voice quivering with deep emotion:

> "'Oh, most happy mansion of the supernal city.
>> Oh, most bright day of eternity, which no night ever obscureth.
>> A day always joyful, always serene, and never changing its state
>>> for the contrary.
>> Oh, that this day would shine forth. It shineth, indeed, for the
>>> saints, resplendent with everlasting brightness.
>> The citizens of heaven know how joyful that day is.'"

Madame's face had gradually brightened till it wore a look almost of exultation.

"If he, if they, our children, and their humble friend should have to die by the guillotine," said the Marquis, "it will be a short passage to the eternal brightness."

"And the joyful day," added Madame, "which never changes to the contrary."

"Meantime," said the Marquis, "while announcing to you the worst, I have yet one gleam of hope. That extraordinary personage, Jambe d'Argent, has sent me word by no means to come to Nantes, lest I spoil all. By which I infer that he has in view some final, desperate effort."

"Let us pray for him," cried Madame; "let us besiege heaven with our supplications that his plan may succeed."

And together they passed into the oratory.

Chapter IX

Citizen Premion Meets an Old Acquaintance

WHEN COUNT GASTON de la Roche André was marched from the Revolutionary tribunal to his prison in the Clock Tower, escorted by half a score of pikemen, on the day of his condemnation, he was greeted with fierce denunciations as the slayer of innocents, the oppressor of the poor, the haughty aristocrat, the leader of La Vendée, who had been about to bring his brigands to burn the town and put all honest Blues to death. Gaston's mien was simple, frank, and manly, according to his wont, but his almost boyish face had an added touch of dignity, for sorrow is ennobling. In his whole carriage was the grace and simple elegance that usually comes of long descent and gentle breeding. One woman alone in the crowd bent her head as he passed. Perhaps she had sons of her own, or possibly she had received, in happier days, some kindness from the family of Roche André.

Premion remained in his room the rest of that day. He had not wished to appear so conspicuously in the trial of Gaston de la Roche André, and he was very much exercised, too, over a letter which he had just received. It threw out hints that Richard Duplessis might not be dead after all. Now, the sudden and somewhat mysterious death of the prisoner of the Clock Tower had been a fearful blow to the lawyer. He felt that he had been balked of the full sweetness of revenge. He had intended that Richard should die, but not until he had drawn out a lingering confinement, tortured by the thought of Jeanne in the power of his rival—not until his character had been blackened in the eyes of Jeanne by charges of treachery toward the Roche Andrés.

This anonymous letter, therefore, roused Premion to a pitch of excitement which threatened to bring on a seizure, and reminded him of the fact that the ex-valet, whom he trusted implicitly, and to whom he had confided various important commissions, had not been seen since the burial of Duplessis, nor could any trace of him be discovered. He had hastened to Premion with the news of Richard's illness, had begged permission to bring a doctor, and had seemed animated by a very passion of republican zeal. It was upon him the lawyer had relied to secure from Richard some statement which might be distorted into an accusation against the Roche Andrés.

The darkest suspicions concerning his late confederate began now to take root in Premion's mind. It was clear that he had been a traitor, and had planned not Richard's ruin, but his rescue, and he, Morin-Premion, had been the dupe and the tool of an impostor. While he was full of the anger and bitterness of this discovery, a woman came to the door, and, her knock remaining unanswered, opened it and entered with a basket of clothes. Premion roared at her to get out of the room, and as she retreated, laying down her basket, he seized her by the arm and rudely pushed her, so that she came within an ace of falling down the stairs, which were just outside.

"You may push me, Citizen Premion," said the woman, turning half way down the steps to flash back defiance at him, "but your own turn will come, and when you fall few, indeed, will mourn."

"Begone, beldame!" he cried fiercely, "or I shall send you on one of Citizen Carrier's pleasure boats to help with his underground fort."

This was in allusion to what were called the *noyades*, a system devised by this monster of the Revolution to destroy, at one blow, a whole cargo of priests and aristocrats.

"If you do send me there," said the woman, with a scornful laugh, "I will be in better company than you ever were in in your life. But I should think you had deaths enough on your soul."

"You shall answer for this insolence at the tribunal," roared Premion.

"The last fish you caught in your net ought to have been enough for you—the son of the man who fed your mother when she was starving, and aided her to educate you."

Premion was silent, partly from rage, partly from astonishment, that this woman should know these hidden pages of his history.

"Then there was Richard Duplessis, who one time saved your life. But he has escaped you."

There was something almost triumphant in this last expression.

"And now you are plotting to get into your power, to send, for aught I know, to death, the betrothed of Monsieur Gaston and your own sweetheart."

With these words she flew quickly down the remaining stairs, while Premion sprang furiously forward, and would have followed her. But an instinct of prudence restrained him. The woman might be armed. The fate of Marat, "friend of the people," was still fresh in his mind. She turned on the last step and threw back at him a final look of mockery.

"Have you asked the Citizen Landriot, the ex-valet, to explain the cause of Duplessis's death?" she asked. "He will live to marry his sweetheart yet, who belongs rightfully to him, and see you dance to Mother Guillotine's tune."

Premion sprang furiously down the stairs.

"Seize that woman," he shouted angrily to two or three men who stood lounging about. "She is a royalist spy, a foe to the people, dangerous to the nation."

The men were listless, some of them seeming but little interested, for these hourly arrests had grown monotonous. Premion himself gazed anxiously up and down the street, but the woman had disappeared as completely as if the ground had opened and swallowed her. The lawyer, much disquieted, returned to his room, where he passed a sleepless night. Twice that day a hint had been given him, and, as he supposed, from two different quarters, for he could not know that his mysterious visitor of the afternoon had written the anonymous letter.

.   .   .   .   .

It was early morning, and as Morin-Premion threw open the window, the dawn was flushing with a soft rose pink the glossy, frowning walls of that town, wherein such crimes were daily being perpetrated. Then memory played the villain who looked forth a strange trick. He thought he was a boy again, and his mother was preparing him for First Communion. They lived alone together, just the two of them, and they were very poor. The mother was weeping because they had no food in the house. Thin and wan, he could see her now looking down upon him with pitiful eyes.

Then the Marquis had come in, like some fairy godfather, and given them gold and sent provisions from the castle, and arranged for his, Morin-Premion's, education. And now he was sending that man's son to the guillotine. Again, he remembered a day when Madame had questioned him at school, and had bestowed on him a prize for his quick answers. The prize, a watch, lay now unused in his case, and its former owner possessed a far more costly one. But vividly, as a flash, came the feeling he had then experienced of intense gratitude toward that high-born lady who had seemed to him then to belong to another sphere. And it was her first-born he was sending to the scaffold.

He leaned far out of the window, for the morning air was cool on his face, fevered with the vigil of the night and with all these disquieting thoughts. But under the blue of the sky he saw only Saint Lyphar and these people who had belonged to his own youth. He recalled a certain occasion when a beautiful young lady had ridden past him upon a snow-white palfrey. He had thought her then the fairest creature in all God's wonderful creation, and as high above him as the stars, and she had smiled at him and thanked him so prettily when he had opened a gate for her. And now she was to be dragged from a loathsome dungeon, to be flouted by evil men, and to die on the guillotine if it so pleased him. He wished for one brief instant that he could save them all. Then the thought of Duplessis occurred to him, his implacable hatred of the man burned up, and he steeled his heart.

He remembered swiftly every schoolboy encounter in which Richard had been victorious, the open preference which Jeanne Dumartin had shown for him, and the favor of the young Count. In Duplessis's defense, Count Gaston had given him a blow, and for that blow he should die. As for the beautiful lady, well, she had chosen her lot. Let her die with her lover. And Jeanne—the guillotine should have her, too, unless he could himself secure her or be assured of Duplessis's death. He dressed himself then, and wandered aimlessly through the streets for hours, turning his feet at last in the direction of the Place de la Guillotine, where crowds, particularly of women, were already hurrying. He took up his station just outside the door, where he could see what went on without being seen. The women, as they passed, called out inviting him to come forth to the festival of the Republic.

"There is a splendid cartful, Citizen," cried one; "priests, nuns, a noble or two, a republican who was caught helping a priest escape, and, best of all, the young Count and his sweetheart. He is a handsome fellow, this Roche André. I wish, instead of killing all these fine-looking aristocrats, they would find them wives among the Blues, the daughters of the Republic."

There was a shriek of laughter at this sally, in which Premion forced himself to join. His quick eye suddenly caught sight of the woman who had derided him but yesterday. He was certain of her identity, though she was differently attired. She stood in the shadow of the building, a proud, cold look upon her face as though she scorned those about her. Premion, in watching her, scarce noted an old man, clad as a country rustic, with long, shaggy black hair falling over his shoulders and a general air of rural simplicity about him. He seemed, indeed, utterly out of place in those wild surroundings.

Though Premion had allowed the countryman to pass unnoticed, the latter, more vigilant, had observed the lawyer in the wine shop, and he had listened to the banter of the women of the people. One pair of eyes, however, dwelt curiously upon the countryman. They belonged to the woman who had reviled Premion upon the stairs of his hotel. Her lips were parted in a scornful smile, but whether the smile was directed against the wily lawyer, whom she, too, had seen, or the simple rustic, who can tell?

"*Citoyenne*," said the woman near her, "the bell of Saint Giles yonder is ringing two o'clock. There are two hours to wait."

"One could wait four for the pleasure we shall have," said the other, and she let her gaze follow that of her neighbor to the tall steeple in the distance, just touched by the sunlight, and whence the bell pealed forth the hour.

"It will be a merry sight," said the first speaker; "above all, Citizen Roche André, with his sweetheart, and the woman Dumartin."

The listener's face darkened at the mention of this last name.

"That is one who shall die!" she muttered. "I will see to that. I will follow the cart step by step, and I shall not lose sight of her for the twinkling of an eye. Richard Duplessis shall lose his fine sweetheart, who consorted with aristocrats and preached to her equals."

As she spoke she fixed her eyes upon the rustic, almost as though she were addressing him, and continued her meditations.

"As for the Count, I would have him live, if I could, and he might have the wax doll to whom he is betrothed. And the nuns and priests, I would save them, too. Once I, too, used to kneel to a priest, and tell my sins, and believe his words of pardon and peace, and, oh, God! I was happy."

It was well for her that during this strange soliloquy her companions were too much absorbed in what was going forward, eagerly lending their voices to the tumult of shouts, cries, laughter, and jests. So that it was only the rustic who gave her his attention.

"You scorned me once, Richard Duplessis," she went on, in the same fierce monologue; "you preferred to me a pudding-faced wench who might have driven the plow. She is giving her life to save you. Be it so. Once I would have given mine."

She broke off with a half sob which did not escape the notice of the observant countryman.

"They tell me there will be heads struck off today!" he said, suddenly addressing her, with the same air of clownish simplicity.

"Yes; beware that yours is not among them," was the strange and startling reply. But the rustic was not to be moved.

"You were weeping, good mistress," he said.

"Faith, not I!" answered the woman proudly; "I tell you again, beware, or you will have cause to weep."

"I came from the country to see the sights," the man went on, imperturbably.

"From the seashore, perhaps?"

There was no mistaking the flash of surprised intelligence which shone for an instant in the eyes of the rustic. Then the eyes were veiled, and he replied:

"From Morbihan way."

The woman bent toward him quickly and hissed in his ears:

"'Tis a lie. And if you are here for the purpose I suppose, I will denounce you. For there is one of the prisoners who must die."

"*Ma foi*, it seems to me there are many," said the rustic, with a shrug.

"The others may drown or be shot, or stay alive, for all of me," cried the woman.

"And that one in whom you, *Citoyenne*, are interested?" inquired the rustic, slowly.

"That one is Jeanne Dumartin. Tell Richard Duplessis from me, a woman of the people, from me, Thérèse Duval, that it is because of him I shall pursue her relentlessly to the foot of the scaffold. She has risked her life for him. He may now risk his in a vain effort to save her. But I shall be there, and he shall not succeed."

"But I have heard talk in the crowds here of this Richard Duplessis, who is a leader of the brigands, and it is said that he died in prison."

A low laugh broke from the woman, but she said no more, for at that moment Premion, issuing from the wine shop, laid a detaining hand upon the shoulder of Thérèse Duval.

"You will come with me and explain your words of yesterday," he said, "and, if they do not bear explanation, to the tumbril with you! It will give a spice of variety to see a knitter of the guillotine occupying a place in the nation's chariot."

Thérèse looked around, disconcerted for the moment. She had forgotten the lawyer on whom she had determined to keep watch. Her eyes sought those of the rustic, but he had disappeared. She stood a moment uncertain, Premion meanwhile scanning her face with attention.

"I have seen you before," he declared.

"You all but threw me downstairs some hours ago."

"Before that, again."

"Your memory is a good one, and your eyes see far back. Perhaps it's as well they don't see too far ahead."

"Cease your chatter," said Premion, angrily. "Whoever you may be, you are my prisoner now. Come with me to the wine shop. If you can satisfy me there, you go free. If you can not, then to the guillotine."

"Thank you, sir, for your promises," she said, with a mocking curtsy.

"Sir me no sir. I am simple Citizen Premion."

"A nice citizen, too, and, as you say, simple, to be tricked," cried the woman, saucily, "by an ex-valet, and——"

It was on her tongue to say that he was about to be tricked again, but an inexplicable something stopped her. The thought of Count Gaston's gallant bearing yesterday at the tribunal, and of the lovely young creature at his side, came back to her.

"I will look out for Jeanne!" she said to herself, "even should Jambe d'Argent succeed in freeing the others, and what else is he here for, dressed like a countryman?"

"What are you muttering?" asked Premion, who, consumed with speechless rage, had been staring at her furiously.

"I am saying that you must not keep me too long from the guillotine. See, I have my knitting here."

She pointed to a bag at her side.

"And I want to put in a stitch for Jeanne Dumartin, at least."

A quiver of uncontrollable agony passed across the man's face. He began to feel that he was indeed powerless to save Jeanne. In this had culminated his long indecision. The woman read his countenance with one swift glance.

"You want to save her," she said; "but I tell you she must die."

"Why are you so intent upon her destruction?" asked Premion, with an impulse of curiosity.

"The same reason which made you desire the death of Richard Duplessis," answered the woman.

Premion started. This woman was endowed with a fearful insight into the hearts of others. Besides, it was evident that she knew something of his history. He drew her hastily into the wine shop, which was just then untenanted.

"Who are you?" he demanded suddenly.

The woman gave a careless laugh. "Why should I conceal it? You may, perhaps, remember Thérèse Duval!"

"And are you she?" cried Premion in amazement.

"You may well ask," Thérèse said, with a defiance which was not without a tinge of sadness.

"The village beauty!" exclaimed Premion. "Why, I was one of your admirers myself."

"Before you met Jeanne Dumartin," Thérèse assented, composedly. "But let that pass. I cared as little for you or your admiration as the flower cares for the butterfly that flutters by."

Premion bit his lip.

"I was, as you say, the village beauty," continued Thérèse Duval. "I had every clodhopper in the place at my feet. There was but one I wanted, and it is that one about whom so much love and so much hate now center—Richard Duplessis."

"Curse the fellow!"

"Yes; curse him if you will. He scorned my advances, made light of my prettiness, and from the first threw himself with the devotion which only such strong natures can feel at the feet of Jeanne Dumartin. He was her slave, her call-boy, her very shadow."

She paused, the full bitterness of what she said reflected in her face.

"And mark you, Citizen Premion, the girl loved him devotedly. She is giving her life for him, and I——"

Her voice broke and ended in a wail of anguish.

"I am striving to deprive him of the sweetness of that love. For you have missed your aim, Morin-Premion. Richard still lives, and I rejoice at it. But with regard to the girl, I shall not fail, I warn you."

Premion stood very white and still. At last his dry lips framed the words:

"If Duplessis lives, I have not the wish, any more than the power, to save her."

The sound of tumultuous shouting just then reached their ears.

"Quick, let me go; they are coming!" said the breathless woman.

"You shall not go till all is made clear," said Premion, resolutely. "I have heard you utter treasonable words. You have guilty knowledge of some of these traitors. I have, therefore, the right to detain you."

"Detain me!" she cried fiercely. "I tell you I must follow the tumbril, as a sleuth hound follows its prey, lest one chance of escape should offer."

"And yet," said Morin-Premion, "I shall detain you till you have satisfied my curiosity. It wants half an hour of the time yet. Begin your story at once, and then I shall judge whether you may attend the tumbril or not."

It was a glance very like hatred which shone from Thérèse's black eyes, but she suddenly changed her tactics.

"To begin, then," she said, seating herself, "I spent my girlhood at Saint Lyphar. Is the Red Inn still there, and does it change in the glint of the morning sun and the glow of the day's decline, and does Père Michel still sit by the church door and ask for alms, Morin-Premion, and pray for us who pray not?"

Premion shrugged his shoulders, indicating by a gesture that he did not know.

"I believe he is a saint," she said, "and, perhaps, a prophet, for he spoke to me, oh, such words, and he said he would pray for me and save me in spite of myself."

"The eternal feminine," said Premion, with a sneer; "always sentiment when there should be action, and behind that sentiment betimes the nature of a tigress."

"And a tigress you shall find me, Premion," said the woman, suddenly dealing him a heavy blow with a walking stick which had lain unnoticed beside her chair. When he recovered himself the woman had gone, and he heard her mocking laugh coming back to him distinct from all that discordant chorus of voices, every moment drawing nearer.

At one of these shouting, swearing bands, who were hastening with wild cries to the Place de la Guillotine, Thérèse put herself. The fever of blood was in the maddened faces about her, the fury of destruction was in those staring eyes and the haggardness of sunken cheeks. They cried out for the blood of the aristocrats, they sang mad songs, they waved their pikes above their heads, holding banners covered with blasphemous or ribald sentences, they tossed red caps into the air, or waved their arms as if calling down the vengeance of the gods.

Of a sudden they were brought to a halt. They had come to the turn of a narrow street, where the houses were close together. Directly in their path, effectually obstructing the way, was a broken-down cart. Beside it, in a posture of uncontrollable grief, was a young lad. His head rested on a broken rail, and he sobbed aloud, while near him stood an elderly man, who also seemed as if he had come down from the country. He was looking at the youth with a piteous expression of grief and concern.

The most surprising sight of all, however, and one not often seen in those days in the streets of the town, was a gentleman, richly clad, with breeches and waistcoat of ruby satin, a surcoat of finest cloth, silken stockings, and shoes with silver buckles.

His appearance raised a shout of execration, and the mob were further infuriated by having its progress stopped. Those in the front began to hurl curses at the head of the unfortunate wagoneers, while those in the rear, not knowing what the stoppage meant, pressed on tumultuously.

"Kill them all, and break up the cart for firewood," cried several voices.

"Down with the aristocrat!" shouted others. "Let him take a drive in the national chariot."

The woman Duval, hurling herself forward, made a movement to strike at the gentleman, screaming:

"You! you!"

Her voice failed her from very rage, and, meanwhile, the gentleman, who stood calm and composed before them, raised his hand for silence and began to speak. Involuntarily, all were silent, so commanding was his mien, so strong the force of character which lit up his fine face.

"Citizens all, and you, fair ladies, in particular," he began.

"There are no ladies here, traitor," cried Thérèse; "they are having their heads frizzed for the guillotine."

"Let me speak a few words to you," said the gentleman, disregarding the interruption. "Here are two worthy citizens, like yourselves of the people, friends to the Republic, who have come to town expressly to see today's sights, and have brought with them such produce as they had, hoping to make some small profit. Hearing your cries, they were hurrying toward the guillotine when this accident happened. I chanced to pass by, and I could not help feeling compassion for this unfortunate youth. He can not raise the horse himself; his shafts are broken; his father is too feeble. Will you not give him your aid?"

"Not now," shrieked some. "We must go on. We may be late."

"But you can not go on without much difficulty unless you clear the way," urged the gentleman.

"This is a traitor, a royalist, an enemy of the people," cried Thérèse, who had several times striven to interrupt the gentleman's discourse. "It's a royalist plot to balk the nation of its revenge. Break the cart to pieces."

"Yes; break it, demolish it," roared the mob.

"But I will not allow you to commit so inhuman an act," declared the gentleman coolly, and at the same time drawing his sword from its scabbard. "The first who advances dies."

Pikes were brandished about him, thrust almost into his face. But the cart served as some protection, and none were anxious to court death.

"Who are you," cried a man, "that dares to oppose the will of the sovereign people?"

"I am one who is not to be trifled with," said the gentleman, sternly.

"*Conspuez* the aristocrat, spit upon him!" cried Thérèse, in a very frenzy of fear lest she be too late, and advancing fearlessly she leaped over the cart.

Instantly the gentleman dropped the point of his sword, bowing courteously:

"*Place aux dames!*"

Thérèse could not restrain a glance of admiration. Here was that man, alone, facing a desperate mob, and trusting to his strong right arm and his fertile brain.

"These aristocrats have their qualities," she thought; but instantly she turned upon the crowd.

"Cowards," she said; "can you not do as I have done, and to the *lanterne* with this aristocrat?"

"To the *lanterne!* To the *lanterne!*" echoed the crowds.

"Now, really," said the stranger, "you are tempting fate, my friends, by rushing on me. My sword will give a good account of itself before it is taken, and, my faith, I do not think your consciences are so clean that you should be in such a hurry to meet your Maker."

"He is preaching the old superstition, priestcraft. Kill him! Kill him!" roared the mob. "He is a priest in disguise."

"You are wrong there, Citizens, as you shall find if you come to close quarters," observed the gentleman. "The priest does not usually practise sword play."

"We shall lose the sights if you do not walk over the body of this peasant and his horse!" cried Thérèse; "that is, if he will not move them."

"We shall move them for him, cart, horse, and all," cried the gentleman. "It is the quickest way. So come, now. No trifling. I recommend you to get to work."

The multitude paused for very astonishment, and some of the women laughed aloud, believing it a joke, but others took the matter more seriously.

"'Tis d'Artois himself," they cried. "We are betrayed; he has the foreign troops behind him or he would not dare to show himself."

And looks of abject terror began to show itself upon some of the countenances.

"The Comte d'Artois! The Comte d'Artois!" was whispered from mouth to mouth. "And the Austrians are at his back, and the dogs of brigands, too. Kill the tyrant, the traitor of the false Bourbon breed."

"My friends," said the gentleman, calmly, raising his voice so as to be heard, "once more you are in error. You are bestowing upon me all manner of titles which are far above my deserts. At one moment you declared me to be a minister of God, at the next instant you exalt me to the royal dignity and to brotherhood with the late King Louis of blessed memory."

He deliberately raised the hat which he had but lately replaced upon his head. A wave of fierce indignation broke over the crowd. A herd of wild beasts let loose were less terrible. But the gentleman's voice rose calmly as before in the pauses.

"I may as well tell you at once that I am neither royal nor clerical, a gentleman, with long descent and short purse. I had forgotten that humanity had gone out of fashion when the rights of man were declared. I supposed that fraternity might mean doing a good turn for another now and then, and that liberty might permit those who wished to serve their fellows to do so unhindered."

The biting irony of the words were lost on some of the crowd, but Thérèse, with flaming face, cried:

"He mocks us with fine phrases, this Judas of a d'Artois. Let us make an end of him."

She had stood by in a species of fascination, as if anxious to see the end of the scene, but, above all, anxious to keep a close watch upon the mysterious stranger.

"I might call you by another name," she hissed into his ear, "and so insure your death, but, for the moment, I pause. Try me not too far. The name of Jambe d'Argent would be as a red rag to a bull."

"You were wondrous fair to look upon, Thérèse Duval," said the stranger suddenly, ignoring her words, "when I saw you first in the Red Inn at Saint Lyphar. You had come home from church like any little saint."

The girl reddened, then paled.

"And those eyes have not lost their luster yet," the gentleman went on. "Use their beauty on the side of mercy."

A half smile played about Thérèse's lips. The voice that uttered these words was rarely winning, and flattery has a wondrous power. "If I were you, with such weapons as you have, I would lead this mob to deeds of heroism."

"I can not even lead them to take your life," said the girl.

"Nor would you do so," said the gentleman. "I know you better than yourself, and I will never believe that the lovely maiden of long ago, simple, pure, and innocent as an angel, would incite to deeds of blood."

There was something of significance in his tone which made Thérèse for the first time pause irresolute.

"Love is a mighty power!"

"Hate is stronger."

"Do not believe it," said the stranger. "Hate bears bitter fruit."

"Call it revenge."

"Revenge recoils on its author."

"A woman who has been scorned——"

"Rises far above the reach of scorn by generosity. A woman may die for a man, but sometimes she serves him best by living and suffering for him."

It was a strange duel of words, there in the midst of an excited throng, with the peasants, who had now so far recovered from their stupor as to busy themselves about their cart, volubly explaining their misfortunes to all who would listen. A certain number of the crowd were actually assisting them. Meanwhile, the winning voice and persuasive gesture of the stranger continued to exercise their fascination upon Thérèse, a fascination which had frequently swayed men's minds and made Jambe d'Argent so invaluable a leader. He held now the fiery mind of Thérèse abashed and waning in her fixed resolve, while the men of the pikes, amid jests and coarse laughter, were starting the peasants on their way.

"If a woman, through her agency, were to give a man happiness, would it not be more than life?" he whispered softly, "and in after years would it not come back to him as a holy memory, so that he should bless that woman's name?"

Tears were standing in the woman's eyes.

"If, through her, on the other hand, came the death of his happiness, worse, far worse, than physical death, should he not remember her with loathing, as the black shadow between him and the sunshine?"

Thérèse bent her head.

"You have conquered," she said, gliding silently forth from the crowd she had been leading on, while the gentleman, looking after her with moisture in his eyes, murmured:

"God be praised for the softness of a woman's heart. It is to human life what the spring is to the year. And so, there is our most formidable obstacle conquered, for she alone guessed at our plans."

Thérèse slunk away, gloomily, in the shadow of the buildings.

"Père Michel is surely praying for me," she murmured.

Chapter X

In the Revolutionary Tumbril

EANTIME FROM the Clock Tower dungeon had gone forth another of those dismal cortèges which, notwithstanding their gruesome familiarity, were hailed by the populace with delight. The names had been called to the strokes of the Clock Tower bell. There was an old priest among them, one of that silent army of martyrs which the French Revolution gave to the world. Their fidelity, their incomparable virtues, devotion to duty, self-sacrifice, and heroic deaths, contrast with the unfaithfulness of a few. While the average historian or the clever romancer sneers at the courtier priests, whom he represents to be as unpopular as a certain section of the nobility, he is entirely silent as to that phalanx of heroes who went to death or exile, "unhonored and unsung."

There were nuns who had languished in prison for many days, and looked forward to execution as to a joyful release. Yseult de Breteuil was there, more beautiful than ever in her new pallor, her noble beauty lit by a marvelous enthusiasm. Jeanne stood directly behind her, but by a refinement of cruelty Gaston was pushed to the very back of the tumbril, while beside Mademoiselle stood a black-browed son of the Republic, who had been caught striving to save a priest.

The driver of the cart sat serenely indifferent to the tumult about him. He had driven this cart so many times, and he often grumbled that he was getting tired of these cargoes of aristocrats.

An officer of the National Guard rode silent and taciturn at the head of a small force, which served as escort. But, indeed, a guard seemed utterly unnecessary, for the people crowded about with shrieks and howls of delight, commenting after their coarse fashion upon the inmates of the tumbril, and singling out now one, now another, for their ribald jests, while even from the windows above, which were crowded with spectators all along the line, taunts and jeers were hurled at the unoffending victims of the people's tyranny.

In the multitude surrounding the tumbril, women predominated—old women, tottering upon sticks, young women, laughing, howling, or joining madly in the singing of the "Carmagnole."

Just at the head of the white horses, which, like death's pale horse in the legend, had borne many a one to the grave, were particularly noticeable a man and a woman who, keeping close together, sang or danced in unison. The woman was in the ordinary garb of the women of her class, and the man, whose thin, dark face was lighted by an expression of reckless gaiety, wore his liberty cap, and roared out the "Carmagnole" with a zest which drew all eyes upon him.

"There's a good Republican for you," cried an old woman, taking a few steps herself to the lively tune they sang, "a merry lad, too, with his lass on his arm."

"Out of the way, mother!" cried the dark man, "or the horses will run you down. They don't know a patriot from an aristocrat."

There was a roar at this sally, and the old woman stepped back, the dark man laying a soothing hand upon the bridle rein of the excited horse. All Nantes was in the streets that day. Premion, after his encounter with Thérèse Duval, had betaken himself to a window, whence, pale and trembling, he peeped forth. He dared not make an effort to save Jeanne, even if his hatred of Duplessis would have permitted him to make the attempt. He caught one glimpse of her as the cart passed his place of observation, and Jeanne, chancing to raise her eyes, fixed them upon his face. He felt that he would never forget that glance, though there was no scorn in it now, but a pity mingled with horror. It was as if she had said to him:

"This is your work! These noble lives must fall to glut your vengeance."

A moment after the shrieks of the furies who accompanied it came back harsh and discordant to the watcher's ears, and, at last, they died away in a sullen silence more awful than any sounds, so that Premion went down again into the streets, and hurried on aimlessly, scarce knowing where he went. Meanwhile new insults were every moment hurled at the prisoners. When they were addressed to himself, Gaston smiled with cheerful indifference, his demeanor being that of a gay and cheerful soldier going into battle. But when they were addressed to the priest or the religious, to Jeanne or to his beloved Yseult, the young man's cheek burned and his hand involuntarily sought the side where he had so long worn a sword.

"Softly, softly!" said the old priest, with a smile as bright as though he were going to a banquet; "this is the way of Calvary. We must take no note of its thorns and briers. We are speeding to an unending joy."

"I forgot, Father," said Gaston, bending his head reverently; "but you will not forget us at the place of execution. Give us a last absolution."

"I will open the gates for you with that mystic key," said the old man, placidly, "and one in yonder window has promised to do the like for me."

He did not look up as he spoke, fearing to betray any secrets to the sharp eyes of the Revolutionists, but Gaston, glancing involuntarily toward a small window over a porch, saw a grave face look forth, while a hand was raised an instant. They were drawing near now to the place of execution, though the way was purposely made as long as possible, that the sovereign people might have every opportunity to gaze upon their fallen enemies.

The bell of St. Giles struck the three-quarters after three. It wanted but a quarter of an hour to the time fixed for the carrying out of the sentence, and already the shadow of the guillotine loomed large in that square which had come to be known by its sanguinary name. The tumbril had to pass through an open space where there were no buildings of any sort, and where the crowd was less dense. Suddenly there was a tumult. No one knew precisely how or why. A tall man raised his voice, proclaiming something which, for the moment, caught the attention of the crowd.

Suddenly the driver of the vehicle felt himself pushed from his place. The reins were instantly seized by the young man of the "Carmagnole," who had abruptly abandoned his companions. He sprang upon the cart, declaring that he would drive, as the driver had fallen off—that the guillotine must not be cheated, and that he would drive straight over all who came in his way. It seemed as if a very frenzy of Republican zeal had seized upon him, and the crowd cheered and applauded him to the echo, while he mutely motioned Yseult and Jeanne to crouch down upon the floor of the tumbril, the nuns imitating their example, and the Republican, in some bewilderment, doing the like, so that only Gaston and the old priest remained erect.

The dark man now, chanting once more the "Carmagnole," whipped up his horses furiously. At first the crowd made way for him, crediting his statement, their attention, moreover, being attracted by the tall man in the rear. Suddenly, Premion, who had arrived upon the scene, strolling along in desultory fashion, realized what was happening. He pushed past the tall man in a frantic effort to reach the cart and stop the horses, but found himself opposed by a man of sturdy build, who, by accident or design, stood directly in his path. Premion, in his fury, seized the man by the throat, at the same time raising the cry of a rescue.

Instantly there was a fierce shout, and the crowd attempted to close about the cart, but the tall man gave command to a concealed force under his own orders, which was near at hand, and a passage was cleared for the cart, which tore madly on. Thérèse Duval stood by, and watched and made no sign.

"He has saved her!" she thought, "and I have had my share in saving them all!"

The dark man drove furiously on through the raging mass, while those who had sought to detain him were presently engaged in a curiously half-hearted encounter with the men who had ranged themselves under that mysterious leader.

"Who is he?" began to be whispered breathlessly.

"The Duc d'Enghien!" cried one.

"The Comte d'Artois!" said another.

"The Égalité!" suggested a third.

"No, blockhead, for he is the friend of the people."

"'Tis Jambe d'Argent or the devil," cried a man, who had just received a blow upon the pate from that powerful leader himself which had sent him reeling.

The cry was taken up and hurried from mouth to mouth. That ominous name, so dreaded by the Blues, which inspired a kind of awe even in his friends, paralyzed the energies of the mob.

"It's no use fighting against him," was the cry. "He is a spirit, an *âme damnée* sent to help these aristocrats."

"There you are talking superstition," objected a voice. "There are no spirits, no lost souls. No life beyond this," and the first speaker was terrified, and cowered away, for it was treason then to express a belief in a future existence.

"You are right," said another speaker. "The friends of reason hold no such superstition. This man is just like all the brigands of La Vendée. He fights like a wildcat, talks like a lawyer, and moves about from place to place as if he had wings."

"Some day his wings will be clipped," prophesied a croaking voice, while above all the tumult rose the despairing shouts of Premion.

"Beat them down! Pursue that cart, or it will be too late. The aristocrats will escape. I tell you, they will escape!"

But none paid any heed to him. All were too much engrossed with the wonderful personality of the great leader, about whom the wildest legends were in circulation. There was no one on either side of the Loire who had not heard of him. His fame was in every hamlet. The children whispered his name with terror. And here he was among them, with how large a following they did not know. The fact itself bewildered and terrified them. He, on his part, seemed to be everywhere; the strength of his arm seemed incredible, and his voice rang out like a trumpet call issuing orders, till at last the cart had disappeared altogether from view. Then the tall man quietly withdrew his little force, all of whom seemed to glide away and vanish in the distance.

Premion, raging like a madman, rushed up to the leader of the National Guard, which had been serving as escort, and, partly by the very force of the crowd and partly by contrivance of Jambe d'Argent, had become separated from the tumbril. To him Premion began a long and not too coherent account of what had occurred. But the officer cut him short, intent now only on one thing—the recovery of the prisoners; for he felt certain that, if their rescue was an actual fact, he should himself take his place upon the scaffold, and expiate by the loss of his head an error which was wholly unavoidable.

Premion, then, tottering as a man under the influence of strong drink, made his way to the *gendarmerie* to arrange that a suitable force should be sent in pursuit. But the officials there were disposed to take his story with more than the proverbial grain of salt.

"You are ill, Citizen," said one. "I should be disposed to think you have fever—the fever of patriotism, perhaps. But you are raving. Listen, that is the bell of the Clock Tower sounding out now the hour of execution."

"But I tell you they are gone, they have all escaped!" he cried.

"It is impossible!" cried the incredulous official. "They were well guarded, and the same driver has driven the national chariot ever since the Republic was proclaimed. He is an honest man and a true patriot, and drained off his glass of aristocrat's blood with a relish. Then there were the people besides, who would have torn the aristocrats to pieces rather than let them be released."

"Fools! Madmen!" cried Premion. "The populace was befooled by the art of a knave, and afterward overpowered, and the driver in whom you have trusted drives no more."

"It is not we who are mad," cried the officials, nettled at the epithets. "I think it will be wise, Citizen, to restrain you, if you do not go peaceably home and to bed. You say that Louis Lanterne drives no more. Bah!"

"I maintain it, and I am as sane as the best of you!" declared Premion, trying to speak calmly.

"Who, then, holds the reins and drives the horses of the Republic?"

"Who? The most dangerous man, save one, in all this district."

"And who may that one be?" asked the official with an air of superior wisdom, while those about him grinned and tittered.

"Richard Duplessis!"

At this answer there was a roar of laughter from all the officials.

"But we signed the permit for his burial three days ago."

"The dead has risen."

"Now we know that you are raving, Citizen," they cried.

"Do you know who I am?" asked Premion, fiercely.

"I do not, but I suspect," replied the chief official, with a humorous twinkle of the eye. "I believe you are the last arrival from the madhouse."

"I am Morin-Premion!" cried the infuriated lawyer.

There was another roar of laughter at this.

"We are certain of your lunacy now," said the chief. "You come to us with a story of this kind, and you expect us to believe that you are the most celebrated of Carrier's associates, a man whose sagacity has become a byword?"

"I repeat that I am Morin-Premion!"

The other shook his head.

"A shallow demagogue he may be," he said, "but not such a fool as you."

Premion flushed crimson.

"You shall pay for your insolence," he said, "and may be yourself arrested for complicity, since you have made no effort whatever to defeat this plot."

"Was Richard Duplessis, dead or alive, supposed to have originated this fine plot alone?" asked the other, with a cool disbelief which was maddening to the irritated nerves of the lawyer.

"Not quite," returned Premion; "its details were carefully prearranged by one Jambe d'Argent."

The officials began to look grave. The power of that name was so great that it dominated, to a certain extent, even the Revolutionary tribunals themselves.

"Jambe d'Argent!" muttered one to the other. "He is capable of anything, and what he desires he accomplishes. Perhaps it would be as well to inquire into the matter."

"Inquire, you asses' heads, after you have lost an hour by your stupidity."

And then the official lost something else—his temper, and had the Citizen Premion, whom he did not at all believe to be the person he represented, locked up on a charge of lunacy. But by the time they collected forces and arrived on the scene of the late disturbance, there was no trace of the chariot of the Republic nor the two white horses. There were only excited crowds who told marvelous tales of that day's strange happenings, and of the chasm in the earth which had opened to swallow up the mysterious stranger, whom they now almost feared to name—the redoubted Jambe d'Argent.

Meantime Richard had contrived to get his cartload of the rescued safe outside of Nantes. Needless to say that the tumbril was presently discarded for a less noticeable vehicle. The white horses were sent galloping back with the empty tumbril to carry terror to the citizens of Nantes, many of whom fled before them panic-stricken.

The prisoners were divided into twos and threes, and were presently safely sheltered in one of those resorts almost inaccessible to the enemy, amidst the dense brushwood of the Bocage. These resorts were protected by watchmen, who placed light, portable ladders against the tallest trees, being thus enabled to foresee the approach of any hostile force. Its approach was made known to the concealed by a few notes upon the shepherd's horn. Or the famous windmills on the Hill of Larks, overlooking the Bocage, was made to do sentry duty by certain prearranged settlement of its wings.

Here, then, on the morning following that day which had dawned so tragically, the good old priest, who had accompanied the other prisoners in the memorable drive through the streets of Nantes, said Mass in the shadow of the woods. The day was just breaking, a delicate, limpid blue following timidly on the roseate masses. The snow, which had fallen here and there, gleamed in the trembling of the new light, the trees, touched with hoar-frost seemed as the marble pillars in some vast cathedral, and the worshipers were animated by a fervor indescribable. Richard Duplessis presently took leave of those whom he had rescued, and whom he had yet to see in a place of even greater security, whence they might embark for some happier and less troubled land. Meantime he had a mission to perform at the Red Inn of Saint Lyphar. He was to convey thither news of the rescue. He was, of course, to proceed there with the most absolute secrecy to entrust Erminie with news for the Château de la Roche André, and thence to make his way back again to the little colony of La Bocage.

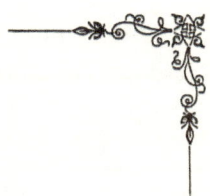

Chapter XI

The Cavern by the Sea

ONE OF THE CHIEF strongholds of Jambe d'Argent, though he had many, was within a rocky cavern hard by the sands of Olonne. Thence he despatched many a cargo of the sand across seas, and thence he not infrequently directed his wonderful plan of campaign by which the men of each village, unless specially called to action, remained there under a local leader, while all were subordinate to one head. Despatches were forwarded by regular system; supplies of provisions collected in various parts of the forest, "the herdsmen were sentinels, the beggars spies, and the women messengers."

It was by means of this plan of action that he had won for himself that wonderful reputation which exalted him almost to the rank of a demi-god, and it was through these various resorts of his, and noticeably by that one on the sands of Olonne, that he was enabled to shelter fugitive priests, religious, and nobles; for there they might abide in safety, no matter how fiercely blew the storms without—material storms, no less than figurative tempests, for the place was a gloomy and forbidding one. Nature had done her best to assist the resourceful leader in securing such a retreat as only the most astute could detect and the boldest seek to enter.

Thither he had transported such of the rescued prisoners as desired to make the journey, while the old priest had preferred remaining where he could minister to the scattered flocks of La Vendée, and the nuns had, at their request, been sent to a house of their order on the confines of Poitou, where they could hope for temporary security. Hence it came about that Jeanne and Yseult, with a venerable lady of Angers who had been the sharer of their rescue as of their condemnation, with Richard Duplessis and Jambe d'Argent, were snugly domesticated in a cavern wherein the hollow sound of the sea reverberated day and night. And there they were momentarily expecting the arrival of the Marquis and Madame de la Roche André, with Gaston, who had gone to seek them. For evil times had come to Saint Lyphar, and a warrant had been issued for the arrest of the feudal lord of that village and his wife. This having come to the knowledge of Jambe d'Argent, he would have sent a trusty messenger to warn them of their danger and offer them an asylum. But Gaston would not be content unless he could go himself.

And so it had fallen out that he had met at the Red Inn of Saint Lyphar, just as the thick darkness of the middle night was settling down on the village, a merchant of small wares and his wife, a comely dame, who had vainly striven to hide her distinction under the mask of coarse clothes.

The afternoon was stormy. Lurid lights glanced over the sands, which gleamed yellow through a mist. At the entrance to the cavern the water restlessly churned among the rocks; a moaning wind swept drearily over the ocean. It wore late, and there was no sign yet of the boat, which should by that time have rounded the point of rocky land, nor yet of the signal rocket which was to proclaim its coming. Richard crept out as far as possible to a point of rock where he could command the open stretch of water and catch the very first sight of the "Marie Antoinette," the trim little vessel which went back and forth upon Jambe d'Argent's errands.

Richard, leaning forward, eagerly strained eye and ear to the uttermost. Only the sound of the waters, the roar of the infinite deep, the screech of the sea-birds broke the silence. Presently, Richard heard a voice behind him. It was that of Jambe d'Argent.

"It grows dark!" he said, and it was evident that he, too, shared those apprehensions which had driven Richard forth from the comfort of the cave, where he loved to watch Jeanne going about her household tasks after her brisk, silent fashion.

"They might have been pursued," Richard conjectured, "and dared not venture thither, lest they disclose this hiding-place."

"It may be as you say," Jambe d'Argent assented. "Maître Julien, who commands the vessel, is a crafty old fox, and will cause Marie to show her heels should danger be in the wind."

After that there was silence between the two men, the strained, intense silence of suspense, in the midst of which they beheld, as some strange portent, the sudden flashing up into the heavens of a red streamer.

"Thank God!" said Jambe d'Argent, fervently.

"Amen!" replied Richard, "for this and all His mercies."

After that there was dead silence for a few moments.

"He will not venture in just yet," said the great leader, calmly, "until he makes sure that his signal could not have been observed by others than ourselves."

As the men waited and listened, there came a noise like the scream of the sea-gull.

"Maître Julien is signaling us again!" cried Jambe d'Argent. "We must display our lights."

And this having been done, Maître Julien, with the practised skill of a veteran mariner, steered carefully between the jagged masses of stone, and was hailed by a joyful though subdued shout from the watchers.

Madame was the first to alight from the craft, leaning upon the arm of her beloved Gaston, and smiling as brightly as though she were arriving at the Château de la Roche André instead of a rocky cave by the sea, whence a vessel would presently convey her and those she loved away from their beloved France. Woman-like, she cared less about the abstract features of the whole terrible situation in France than that her first-born had been saved to her, and that the Marquis and herself had escaped the ignominy of a dungeon, probably the martyrdom of the guillotine. With the Marquis it was otherwise. He saw not only the downfall of his authority and feudal importance, but the downfall of his order. He beheld a cataclysm, where others only saw a flood, which had overflowed its banks, but would return thither again. He looked aged and sorrowful, though he strove to maintain his habitual dignified serenity.

Jambe d'Argent met his guests with the grace of a courtier.

"Madame," he said, "it is a strange and squalid abode to which I have the honor of welcoming you, but for the time being it is your own. And you, Monsieur de la Roche André, consider that you have reached home."

"I thank you, sir," said the Marquis, "but my debt to you is too great and far-reaching for words to touch it."

"It is mine to be grateful for the privilege of serving those I esteem," replied Jambe d'Argent, and, as if to change the subject, he led his guests through winding and rocky passages to a vaulted chamber, illumined by the light of a huge fire. Two girls sprang forward with cries of joy to greet the new arrivals. Yseult, looking more charming than ever in her simple Breton costume, and Jeanne, with her round cheeks, browned by exposure, and her blue eyes, stood looking at them smiling through her tears. Gaston sprang at once to Yseult's side.

"What I have suffered in your absence!" she said. "I feared, I feared you might be recaptured."

"And I have suffered from your absence!" cried Gaston. "The separation was cruel after so late a reunion."

By the light of the pinewood fire which glowed upon the hearth, he gazed tenderly into the young girl's face.

"How beautiful you are, my Yseult!" he cried, enthusiastically—"in this peasant disguise, more enchanting than ever."

Yseult, blushing, answered with her pretty smile and dainty courtesy.

"You are learning to be a flatterer, Monsieur le Comte, and that I will never abide. So I must go and help Jeanne with our supper."

"Not yet, ah, not yet," he pleaded, stretching out a detaining hand.

"But Jeanne is doing all the work."

"Our good Jeanne will not grudge me a quarter of an hour's pleasure."

"It is so delightful, too, to really work and cook for ourselves and serve the table."

"But it is far more delightful to me to hear you talk and sit beside you in the firelight, and realize that we have actually escaped from prison and death, and still have each other."

Yseult's eyes filled with tears.

"Oh, Gaston!" she said, "when we think of it!"

He assumed a lighter tone, to divert her mind from that fearful topic.

"So that is why you should be kind, and stay with me now, and give me this little half hour till the supper is ready."

He spoke with a boyish, winning grace, which was irresistibly attractive.

"You said a *quarter* of an hour before," said Yseult, mischievously; "it is the old story, the more one has, the more one wants."

"That is exactly the case when it is a question of your company."

"I shall really have to go away," said Yseult; "you are such a fine gentleman and a courtier with all those pretty phrases."

And she made a movement to rise from the rude settle by the fire to which Gaston had led her. But he would not let her go, and as he had a very imperious and masterful way with him when he liked, Yseult, yielding gracefully, sat still, smiling at him and looking unspeakably pretty in the firelight.

"I fear you are going to be quite a tyrant, Gaston," she laughed.

"A tyrant and a slave, then, at once," said this ardent lover. "And as to pretty phrases, there are none ever invented that would not apply to you."

Jambe d'Argent had been watching the pair all the while, a smile parting his mobile lips, and a shade of sadness darkening his steel-blue eyes, as he said to Madame:

"If love laughs at locks and bars, it likewise laughs at perils and discomfort. Look yonder, Madame, at the most charming picture of youth and happiness which it has been my good fortune to see for many days. The glow on the cheeks, the light in the eyes, the happy smile! Oh, that is, indeed, a direct legacy from paradise."

Madame looked in the direction indicated. The firelight was shining full on the gallant figure of the young Count, straight and erect as a lance, his eager, handsome face bent toward his beautiful betrothed, who seemed, in the recovered glow of freedom and happiness, radiant with a subtle loveliness which lay not altogether in form or figure. Her brown eyes, delicately arched by darker eyebrows, her reddish-brown hair, and her transparently olive skin made up a picture from which the masters of art might have drawn inspiration. The Marquise, too, smiled and sighed:

"*Qu'il fait beau d'etre jeune!*" she said. "How beautiful it is to be young!"

"And when young, lovely, as Madame will recall," said Jambe d'Argent, with his courtier-like bow. "At the ball of the Embassy, thirty years ago, I remember a picture. Mademoiselle de Saint Germain has just entered the room with her mother. She was clad simply in white, with a nosegay of violets in her hand."

Madame started.

"There were a circle of admirers about her, and I, approaching with difficulty, received a smile, a glance of the eyes, and finally the honor of a dance."

"You were there, and you danced with me?" inquired Madame, in astonishment.

"I was there, and I had that pleasure," said Jambe d'Argent. "You could not possibly remember me any more than you would remember one of the wax tapers which gleamed around, but I, Madame, I was looking at a star. That picture, that smile, that glance I have never forgotten. I am old now, and may dare to speak of these things."

"And an old woman, long unused to flattering words, may hear," said Madame, with her bright smile; "but I pray you to tell me the name of one associated thus with my far away youth."

Jambe d'Argent bent and whispered a name. Madame started.

"That name must never be mentioned aloud in France," the strange man said. "It is dead, dead as our order."

"But Duke——"

"The Duke is dead, too, Madame. Jambe d'Argent lives." And so saying, he bowed and left the Marquise still standing, with an amazed, bewildered look upon her face. Jambe d'Argent now advanced to Richard, casting upon him an amused, inquiring look. He had never exchanged an audible word with Jeanne, although he had continued to catch her eye, and ever and anon, as she came and went about her household duties, he murmured a tender word heard by her alone, a word which sent her with brightened eyes and the glow of a happy light in them about her work.

"Love-making suits you but ill, Duplessis," said Jambe d'Argent. "The clash of arms, after all, agrees with you better."

"Well, at any rate, my lord," said Richard, "love makes a very ass of me. It steals my wits and ties my tongue."

"That organ of yours is never very fluent," said the leader. "You are a man of action rather than of words. But after all that you and she, that all of us, have passed through together, I thought you would have had much to say to the pretty one yonder."

"Jeanne is satisfied," said Richard, smiling, so that the smile lit up his dark face as sunshine upon a rock.

"She looks so," agreed Jambe d'Argent. "Yet she is but a woman. Give your tongue a little more play. Lose your shyness, which makes you hesitate to make love before an audience. Follow the example of your Count. He has done famously, and I could swear has told his beautiful betrothed, with eyes and tongue, a dozen times that she is the sun to his earth."

"I will try to meet your wishes, my lord," laughed Richard, "when Jeanne is not so busy."

"Not my wishes, but hers and yours, you sly dog!" said Jambe d'Argent. "Well, if your tongue is silent, your eyes are eloquent enough, and you have scarce taken them off her."

It was now necessary for Jambe d'Argent to offer his arm to Madame and lead her to the supper table, which he did with as much ceremony as though the cavern had been an ancestral palace, and as though some rude deal boards, roughly put together, had been the banqueting board. The Marquis made his bow to the old lady from Poitou, Gaston following with Yseult, while Richard brought up the rear with Jeanne. Jeanne had proposed to wait upon the guests, but to this none of the company would consent. Distinctions of rank were for the time forgotten, and all agreed to help themselves to the good things put before them. The room was lighted by tallow dips in tin sconces hung about the wall, and a pine torch dipped in oil and placed upon the hearth further illumed the darkness. The table-cloth and dishes were of the coarsest, but never merrier company sat down to banquet. Their appetites were sharpened by the sea air; some had the added zest of a journey by boat.

Their recent danger lent a charm to present security, their partings to present companionship, while the happenings of the last weeks formed an inexhaustible topic of conversation. Added to this the glow that radiated from the faces of four happy lovers, and there was certainly material for a very enjoyable dinner party. So that if the Marquis de la Roche André thought with misgivings of the probable fate of his castle, if Madame sighed to think that she might reign there as mistress and chatelaine no more, if both gave a thought to that other absent son, who was known, however, to be so far safe with Charette and the Grand Army, neither gave any sign. They controlled all emotion for the sake of those about them.

Gaston was in glowing spirits. He felt all the zest of an adventurous spirit for danger and for unusual situations, and he experienced, moreover, the joy of being reunited to the one best beloved. Richard was full of a deep content and thankfulness, and Jambe d'Argent, with a half-cynical tolerance of the love affairs about him and a real pleasure in having made so many people happy, was in the gayest of spirits. But all at once he fell silent, appearing to be lost in thought. Then he rose up, holding a glass of wine in his hand.

"With Madame's permission," he said, "there is one toast I would like to give."

Madame bent her head in assent.

"Let us drink, then, to Thérèse Duval."

Gaston and Richard, deeply moved, stood up. They knew enough of the matter from Jambe d'Argent to feel that she had, in some sense, saved their lives. And Monsieur le Marquis, standing up likewise, courteously drank a toast, the meaning of which he did not understand.

"To Thérèse Duval, then!" cried Jambe d'Argent.

"To Thérèse Duval!" cried the others.

"Vive Thérèse Duval!" added Gaston.

Richard, deeply moved, drained the glass in silence. Then followed a few words of explanation, and, put in Jambe d'Argent's terse and dramatic style, it was a moving incident. It was necessary to suppress facts, to omit details, but when the story was told tears were streaming down the face of Jeanne, while Yseult, the Marquis, and even the old lady from Poitou were visibly affected.

Jambe d'Argent told them, at the company's request, many incidents of his life. Some were so strange and so striking that their weirdness seemed to match the surroundings, the booming sea without, the stony walls within, and the echoes of the various voices resounding through the rocky windings of that subterranean retreat.

"Once," he said, "I had been on board a vessel, in the earlier days of the Revolution, with a prince of the royal blood, later beheaded at Paris. We had put in at a port, which we supposed to be safe, for refreshments, when we were detained by an officer of the National Guard, who made all on board prisoners. As the prince stepped out of the boat, I thrust my hat down firmly over my forehead, and spoke rudely and commandingly to him.

"'Pass on, proud aristocrat!' I cried. 'Though in your service and bound by necessity to follow you, it is a happy moment for me that I see you humbled. I shall see you further punished for your crimes against humanity.'

"One of our men, the gallant young Count de Polinière, jumping up, confronted me:

"'Be silent!' he cried; 'for very shame, be silent! You have been specially favored by his Highness. You have eaten at his table, and pretended friendship for him. Do not dare to address him thus. You are a disgrace to our order.'

"I took no notice whatever of the fiery young gentleman, and his Highness took no notice whatever of me. His fine figure, stooped more from care and grief than from years, was particularly impressive in those surroundings. Perhaps he guessed my motive, for he had honored me with his notice, and had admitted me to intimate friendship, or, perhaps, he did not deign to notice an attack which in baseness rivaled that of Judas.

"The National Guardsmen themselves maintained a silence which I felt to be disapproving, for the Revolutionary fury had not then spread its madness through the land. A young man upon the shore took off his hat and cried, 'God save your Highness!' unrebuked by them.

"It was altogether a singular scene, even in the life of a man who has passed through many strange ones, and I ran a double risk, for, did the *sans-culottes* suspect me, I should have been certain of a quick death, while, on the other hand, were we to fall in with loyal troops, I had been convicted as a traitor.

"Once we were ashore, I pushed my way about so insolently and aggressively, *ma foi*, they must have thought I was Égalité himself. I gave such damning evidence against my late benefactor that I rose at once to the position of confidential adviser to the President of the nearest tribunal, whither we were speedily hurried.

"The prisoner was given almost entirely into my charge. I did not inform him by look or sign of the reasons for my conduct through prudential motives, and I had occasion to admire the patience and magnanimity of the man, who never once reproached me with my ingratitude.

"Well, one night his Highness and I spent a few uncomfortable moments, in extreme peril of our lives, descending from a high tower on a rope in the darkness, and next morning the jailer found a stuffed figure wearing the clothes of his Highness. It sat with head bowed over the table, and on his first visit he did not perceive the exchange. When he did so, the hue and cry was raised and echoed far and wide, but my faithful Julien was waiting with the light-heeled bark 'Marie Antoinette' at the shore, and Monseigneur supped with me, in this very room, sitting where you, Monsieur le Marquis, now are."

There was a pause. The shadows in the corners of the cavern seemed stirred by these memories rather than by the dancing firelight. Jambe d'Argent said, after an interval, musingly, as though his thoughts were upon that bygone scene:

"I have played many parts in my life, but never one, I believe, to such perfection as that of a renegade to my order and a denouncer of the vices of nobility."

Some one asked:

"What became of the gallant young Count and the others?"

"Happily for themselves," said Jambe d'Argent, "they were released, for lack of evidence against them, before my little adventure with Monseigneur. Men were not then so bloodthirsty as they have since become, and some form of trial was accorded."

Here the sound of a rude song reached the ears of the company. The Marquis started, and even Gaston half rose, with his hand to his sword. Jambe d'Argent smiled:

"It is Julien and the rest of my men making merry in the adjoining cavern."

And their song was somewhat as follows:

"Ho, ho! ice and snow!
Summer and Spring,
Winter and Fall,
We merrily sing,
'God bless the King!'
Confusion and woes
Fall on his foes!
God bless the King!"

This chorus was followed by the singing, in a rich tenor voice, of a love song, which ran thus:

"The maiden, the maiden I love,
She has sun-bright hair and a smile without guile,
A cheek like the rose and an eye like the sloe!
Here's to her whom I love!
May the saints above
Keep that beautiful maid from harm!"

The song fell with a tender cadence upon the little group, which, leaving the table, had clustered round the fire, and looks and smiles were exchanged by four young people, and a tender melancholy stole over all. Gaston, snatching a pewter goblet from the table, sprang to his feet and joined in the refrain:

"Here's to her whom I love!
May the saints above
Keep that beautiful maid from harm!"

He ended with a gallant bow to Yseult, who blushed rosily.

"Bravo, Count!" cried Jambe d'Argent. "I like to see a man gallant in love, as fiery in war."

Gaston laughed gaily and replaced the goblet on the table.

"You shall have three days of this monotonous dwelling and peasant fare," said Jambe d'Argent; "we must devise some means of passing the time pleasantly, and music is one of them."

"This, by the way," said Gaston, "is no peasant's beverage; it is a Burgundy of the finest bouquet."

"You are right, but it goes ill with our unsavory viands," said Jambe d'Argent; "but we have eaten with cheerful hearts."

"And given God thanks for His mercies!" said the Marquis.

"Amen to that!" cried all present, and at the moment they heard over the roar of the surges the faint, distant sound of a bell.

"'Tis the Angelus ringing beyond there," said Jambe d'Argent, and immediately he knelt reverently, all present following his example, requesting Madame to recite the prayer.

"They are saying it within," he said, when he had arisen again, and all stood listening to the hum of rude voices in the adjoining cavern. "We need to keep the blessing of God about us, and none here neglects night or morning to invoke that benediction."

Chapter XII

The Red Inn Once More

THROUGH ALL the stormy times that had come to Saint Lyphar, the Red Inn still reared its head, catching the reflection of the sun at morning, and glowing under the warmth of the sunset. Maître Dumartin still presided there as of yore, and heard within his tap-room noisy and vehement denunciations of aristocrats in general, and the family of Roche André in particular. Dumartin listened, saying little, for he knew remonstrance was useless, and even dangerous, but in his heart he had an unchanging love and reverence for the old feudal lords, who had done so much for Saint Lyphar. He heard foreign agitators denouncing the vices of nobility, but he knew that the people of the chateau had been models of every virtue, as was, indeed, the case with the Breton nobility in general.

He was very lonely, Jeanne not daring to return to Saint Lyphar. She had gone with the exiled family of Roche André to England, where her marriage to Richard Duplessis had followed upon that of Count Gaston and Yseult Breteuil, both young wives being virtually widowed by the departure of their husbands for La Vendée to fight once more in the ranks of the Catholic army. Erminie, too, was married and living at Nantes. She visited her father frequently, and often laughed over the day when she had danced the "Carmagnole" with Richard beside the Revolutionary tumbril, in order that he might be near when the moment came to secure the vehicle.

One evening Dumartin sat alone, cowering over the fire and pondering gloomily on all that he had heard. A low knock was heard at the door, and as the innkeeper answered it a tall but boyish figure, wrapped in a cloak, stood upon the threshold. As he advanced into the room, Dumartin cried in a voice of suppressed excitement:

"Merciful heaven! Count Robert, is it you, or one from the dead?"

"It is I," said the other, his serious face relaxing into a smile.

"But we heard you had fallen with the brave General Bonchamp at Saint Florent."

"I fell, but I got up again, thanks to the loyalty of a peasant who concealed me in his hut. Ill of my wounds for a long time, I came here, to find the chateau untenanted, and have so far been unable to discover any trace of my family. Speak, Dumartin, speak! They can not have perished. God is too good to permit an angel like my mother to fall into the hands of those demons."

"They are all safe, Monsieur," cried the honest innkeeper, a smile overspreading his good-humored face, "safe as can be, and away in England, save Count Gaston, who is fighting with General Charette. The Count has been taking a wife, too. You can guess who that would be!"

"Mademoiselle de Breteuil?"

"The same. And my Jeanne is with them, and is the wife of another officer in the Catholic army—Richard Duplessis."

"Richard Duplessis, our old friend," cried Count Robert, "who has become a great hero. His praises are on every tongue. I have heard much of him. But how did they all reach England?"

"It is a long story, too long to tell now," said Dumartin. "Count Gaston, Jeanne, and Mlle. de Breteuil were rescued from the tumbril which was taking them to the guillotine, and Richard was also got out of prison, all through the doings of that supernatural being, that Jambe d'Argent."

"Jambe d'Argent!" cried Robert, raising his hat. "God bless that gallant gentleman, one of the noblest of all that gallant host that has risen in La Vendée."

"He is uncanny," muttered Dumartin; "most likely he is a spirit."

"The spirit of enterprise, of daring, of heroism!" cried Robert.

"And now, Monsieur, what am I to do with you? You can not stop here. Citizen Premion is to address a number of men tonight, in this very room, and his theme is to be the destruction of the Château de la Roche André. Some say he will not permit them to destroy it entirely, but just enough to satisfy the people, while he will come back when all is safe and live there."

"The scoundrel!" cried Robert.

"Scoundrel he is, and, if he found you here, your life would not be worth the snuff of yonder candle."

"But where shall I go?" asked the young man, helplessly.

The innkeeper shook his head.

"There are few places safe for one of your name in Saint Lyphar," he said. He stopped, as if in deep thought, then all at once cried out:

"I have it! There is a shaft for grain in my barn. I will let you down into it by means of a rope, and there you can remain in safety for a time. I will come for you, do not fear, whenever I can do so without danger, and you can enter the inn for food and rest. Come with me now, instantly, for I fear Premion."

They went out together. It was still the dim twilight of summer. Dumartin and the younger man stood regarding the aperture in the shaft which was soon to be his hiding-place, and Robert was about to attempt the descent, when a shadow fell across the floor. Dumartin started guiltily, and Robert put his hand to the place where his sword had been. It was no longer there, because from motives of prudence he had discarded it, removing all traces of his military profession before venturing into Saint Lyphar. Next moment an old man, who had a quite decrepit appearance, stood upon the threshold, leaning upon his stick and regarding them.

"Alas!" cried Dumartin, "we are lost!"

"What is lost?" asked the visitor in a muffled tone. "You and the young gentleman have some interest in the shaft. We will not say what that interest is, and I——"

"And you, Citizen—I mean, Monsieur—I don't know what I mean," stammered poor Dumartin, flurried.

"I want to give Count Robert de la Roche André a rendezvous for tomorrow morning in the parlor of the Red Inn."

"What, you know him?" cried the innkeeper.

"Since, sir, you are aware of my name and quality," said Count Robert, "I will ask you to explain why you desire to give me rendezvous?"

Robert had much of the gravity and impressiveness of manner which characterized his father, the exiled Marquis, whom he resembled much more than he did his mother.

"You may trust me without explanation," said the old man. "I may have to ask you, sir, to accompany me upon a little journey."

"Whither?"

"To a certain seaside resort near the Sands of Olonne, where I once had the pleasure of entertaining some other members of your family."

"You are, then——" cried Robert, stepping forward.

"No names," interrupted the other. "I wear this wig, these signs of age, this air of decrepitude for a purpose, and that purpose is to be unknown."

"The seashore! The pleasure of entertaining!" Dumartin muttered. "Merciful powers! it must be Jambe d'Argent himself."

His fear and agitation were so great that he came within an ace of falling down the shaft.

"And you, Dumartin," said the mysterious visitor.

"Yes, your Mightiness,—your Worship,—your Highness!" cried the innkeeper, his knees knocking together in his terror, and his eyes distended with fright.

"Tush, man! Your love of titles is enough to send you and me both to the guillotine. Should anyone inquire about me, I am old Dr. Dubois, hark ye, Dumartin, old Dr. Dubois, decrepit and childish."

"Yes, Dr. Gobois."

"If you remember everything else as well as you remember my name," laughed the old man, "there is no possible danger of mistake. Therefore, I beg you, too, Count Robert, to take note of my instructions."

He drew near in order to repeat them impressively, and Dumartin, seeing his approach, deftly changed his position in order to put Count Robert between him and the formidable visitor. He watched him uneasily from under his bushy eyebrows all the time he was speaking, and when by accident or design the stranger put his hand upon his shoulder, he executed a very neat somersault, and arrived somewhere near the door. The old man, laughing at the mishap, and with a parting gesture urging caution, turned away, and was soon lost to sight in the gathering darkness.

Dumartin, then arising from his recumbent position, aided the young gentleman down into the shaft, where he was to remain until Premion's meeting was over, and that demagogue had taken his departure for Nantes, as he had announced his intention of doing. Dumartin made his way back to the house very gingerly, starting at shadows and executing quite a variety of steps in his constant apprehension of another meeting with the terrible Jambe d'Argent. Dumartin was scarce back at the inn when Premion entered, saluting the host with a mocking bow and a taunting address.

"Have you had news from your pearl of a daughter? How she did cheat Dr. Guillotine! Perhaps he may get another chance at her some day. I should like to see her upon the scaffold with her husband."

He made an expressive gesture, while his face grew dark with a scowl of fiendish hatred, which caused Dumartin to tremble, while Premion went on.

"Her husband, the traitor, Duplessis, the slave of priests, the tool of aristocrats! Some day I shall hold him in my power, and then he shall burn at a slow fire. Perhaps, if the widow has grown old, I may throw her in, too, as they do in India. If still young, why, she may be mine after all."

He laughed with diabolical malice. Dumartin furtively crossed himself.

"He is possessed, this man," he thought; "he has sold himself to the devil."

"Meantime, I don't know why I keep your head from falling into the basket. You are a traitor, Dumartin, a friend of aristocrats. Your daughter and your precious son-in-law are traitors. Once I have finished this business of the chateau, I must really have you guillotined."

He marked with glee the unspeakable terror of the innkeeper, and continued to torment him.

"The Red Inn will be a capital berth for one of my friends. It has a splendid site. It is really the chief feature of the village, excepting the church, which I intend to have demolished together with the chateau, or turned into a stable."

"Merciful Providence, what are you saying!" cried Dumartin. "Have a care how you blaspheme! Père Michel said, only this morning, that the punishment of blasphemers is awful."

"Père Michel!" Premion thought. "Where had he heard of that man?" Then it came back upon him—from the lips of Thérèse Duval, coupled with a sinister prophecy of evil to himself. A chill crept over him, though the room was warm. Had this Père Michel some power of enchantment? He remembered how Thérèse had come to him on the day after the rescue, and explained why she had failed in her promise to see Jeanne killed.

"Père Michel was praying for me," she had said, "so I could not interfere to prevent a rescue."

Premion turned impatiently to Dumartin, being anxious to rid himself of this memory.

"Cease your insolent chatter, and be careful how you provoke me, or even your good cooking may not keep you alive another week."

Dumartin trembled and was silent.

"Who is this Père Michel?" Premion demanded suddenly, harking back involuntarily to that unpleasant subject.

"The beggar who sits by the church wall."

"Where is he now?"

"Here!" said a muffled voice, and old Père Michel stood before them, a tattered cloak covering his bent shoulders. "I have heard all, and I tell you, Morin-Premion, that the punishment of blasphemers shall fall upon you soon, if you do not change your course."

Even in Premion's mocking laugh could be detected his inward fear—cold, creeping, like that which passes over those of strong imaginations on entering a graveyard. The old man raised his hand with an impressive gesture, as if reminding Premion of God above them. Then he passed slowly to his customary seat in the chimney corner, bending down over the glowing embers, and apparently oblivious of all about.

"This old scarecrow, too, must be shortened by a head," said Premion, looking after him.

"Touch him not! He is a saint!" cried out Dumartin.

"The saints of the Revolution, Citizen," said Premion, "are those who kill most priests and nuns, rob most churches——"

The conversation, to Dumartin's relief, was interrupted by the entrance of a noisy crew, who had come to attend the republican meeting. Then ensued a jingling of glasses, coarse laughter, rude jests, ribald or blasphemous, till Premion rose to speak. He had sat somewhat silent at the table in the center of the room, for over all the din he heard as clear as a bell the words of Thérèse and the subsequent warning of Père Michel. Yet, once on his feet, he hurled defiance at his own very misgivings, speaking with a reckless desperation unusual to him. He denounced more fiercely than ever all that was most sacred, and especially urged upon his hearers the work of demolition, which he would undertake upon his return.

"The chateau shall disappear," he said, "or be given to some brave *sans-culotte*, who will hold it for the nation. The church shall follow. Tyranny and superstition shall fall together."

"Speak on, Citizen Premion," said a voice, "and reck not that the hour of doom is approaching."

Premion started and turned pale. His glance went first to Père Michel, but his head was bent upon his breast in the customary attitude of contemplation.

"Search the room!" commanded Premion.

The room, the outhouses, and the road outside were searched. The Jacobins present, for fear of being themselves suspected, were overzealous in the examination. But nothing was discovered, for old Dr. Dubois had managed to take his departure from the window without in the first movement of surprise and alarm. From a secure hiding-place he laughed at the panic which he had created by assuming the rôle of prophet.

"I argue merely from the logic of events," he said to himself. "The Revolution is already beginning to devour its own progeny. Already many of the most conspicuous Jacobins have fallen. Many more must follow."

Meanwhile in the inn parlor, though all had returned to their seats, conjecture and surmise were blended with a feeling of almost superstitious terror. The wind without seemed to have a voice, penetrating long dead consciences with unspeakable terrors. The crackling of the flames on the hearth had something portentous in its sound, and the figure of old Michel assumed an uncanny aspect. Citizen Premion, braving it out, continued to denounce aristocrats, Moderates, Girondists, to utter horrible maledictions against the clergy and the nobles, until, at last, he rose, lighted a cigar, and took a farewell glass of cognac.

"I shall leave you, good friends," he said, lightly. "I take the midnight express for Nantes, but first I must freshen my wits by the coolness of the night air."

Passing out into the night, he wandered aimlessly hither and thither, desiring to pass the time between that and midnight, for the tumult of the inn parlor had become intolerable to him, and he had read in the scared faces of the men how deeply that mysterious warning had touched them. Whether it was some sound which he heard, or merely the instinct of the bloodhound gaining scent of the prey, it is impossible to tell, but he approached the door of the outhouse where Count Robert lay concealed, and, entering, struck a match. As he did so, he heard a muffled voice, crying:

"Is that you, Dumartin?"

He answered in a feigned voice that it was.

"Then, for heaven's sake, let me come up," complained the voice. "I am cramped and stiff, cold and hungry. I would rather face a score of *sans-culottes* than stay another moment."

"Wait but an instant!" cried Premion, and, returning hastily to the inn, he found there still a dozen or so of the wretches with whom he had lately been carousing.

"There is good sport for us, my children," he cried. "Dumartin has been hiding an aristocrat in his grain shaft. Come till we pluck him out. Tomorrow the inn is yours. Dumartin shall answer at the tribunal for the crime."

The unfortunate innkeeper, deadly pale, stood motionless with terror.

"Tell us whom you have in hiding, my good Citizen Dumartin?" said Premion; "though, indeed, it matters little, for you and he shall go to Nantes in company."

Dumartin extended his hands in supplication, and Premion added in a low, stern voice, intended for Dumartin's ears alone:

"The father's head shall now pay for the daughter's offenses against me." And he passed on, followed by the half-score of

Jacobins, bearing lanterns and making night hideous with their clamor. They presently brought forth the young aristocrat, who, seeing into what a fatal error he had fallen in betraying his hiding-place, maintained a dignified and unruffled composure, which was the almost invariable tradition of his order in these times of social upheaval.

"Your name and station?" asked Premion.

"I know of no right by which you question me," answered Count Robert.

"You shall presently know," retorted Premion; "but you can not deceive me by evasion. You bear in every line of your face the seal of those accursed Roche Andrés. You are the *ci-devant* Count Robert."

There was a howl from the scoundrels who accompanied Premion. Nearly all were strangers to Saint Lyphar, and every man a pronounced Jacobin of the fiercest type.

"Secure this beast of an aristocrat!" cried Premion, "and take him to the Red Inn."

Only once did Count Robert show the slightest emotion, and that was when he beheld the ashen face and trembling limbs of the poor innkeeper.

"Dumartin!" the young man cried, "forgive me for the misfortunes I have brought upon your house."

"It matters not, Count Robert," said the poor man, trying to speak firmly. "I would do the same again, and more, for any of your race."

"You shall have the advantage of going to prison, and probably to the guillotine, for him," sneered Premion. "Secure the old man, too, my brave *sans-culottes*, and to the cellar with him, among his own wine casks!"

The order was obeyed, and presently poor Dumartin found himself securely bound, in the darkness of the cellar, while Count Robert was locked into a small apartment, which served as a larder, with but a grating high up in the wall for a window. At dawn

Morin-Premion set out to take the train for Nantes, having lost the midnight express in the excitement of his great discovery. He declared that he would return in a day or two with warrants for the prisoners, and a sufficient number of Marat men and other true patriots to strengthen their hands in the assault upon the chateau.

"It is yours, true republicans," he said, "since those traitors of nobles have fled the country. It has a rich store of food, of wines, of plate, and jewels. They shall be yours, my children, upon my return."

He set out jauntily from the Red Inn, little guessing that foot of his should cross the threshold no more, and that a Nemesis was waiting for him at Nantes in the shape of the spy whom he had once struck. Meantime the village of Saint Lyphar, as well as that once hospitable and prosperous hostelry, was filled with the scum of neighboring towns, gathering like crows about carrion for the feast of plunder which Premion had promised. They emptied the larder, they drained the wine casks; in their drunken fury they broke the furniture and defaced the walls. The old edifice, battered, defiled, with broken windows and door torn from its hinges, looked the very picture of forlorn age. Dumartin and the young Count were meanwhile fed on the merest scraps of the coarsest food, barely sufficient for their sustenance.

The self-styled patriots scoured the streets, pillaged the farms, whence most of the men had gone to the camp of Grand Bordage. Saint Lyphar had become a horror to itself, with these hordes of bawling ruffians, in red cap, woolen spencers, hoarsely filling the once pure and peaceful atmosphere with the "Carmagnole."

They waited for Premion, but Premion did not come, and at last they made up their minds that they would wait no longer. He was not their master. He had no claim upon the chateau. They would go thither and enrich themselves with all that it contained. They were urged forward to this desperate course by the growing scarcity of food and drink in the neighborhood of Saint Lyphar.

It was a lowering afternoon, gray and threatening, when these demons of discord began to assemble about the castle, which had been so long a place of benediction. The terror was at its height all over France. Law and order had been set at naught, and the fire from burning chateaus mingled with the blood-stained atmosphere, and sent up fearful petitions to offended heaven.

Forth from the inn swarmed the leaders, if leaders any could be called in the motley throng of desperadoes, calling upon all to follow. Up the rocky path they rushed, arming themselves with sticks, with stones, with flails. But a few among them carried firearms. Their dark and evil faces were alight with the passion of greed, the fury of destructiveness. They made battering rams from the stumps of trees, and carried with them barrows, which they had stolen from the farmers, to bear hence the plunder. They raised a wild chanting of the "Carmagnole," and, with a storm of curses and execrations, shook their fists at the grand old pile which rose above them, as though it had been a sentient thing and guilty itself of oppression. Then, with a mad, determined rush, they broke open a postern door and began to bring forth the stores. Suddenly a stern voice rose above the tumult.

"Jacobins! Friends of liberty!" it said. "You have been waiting for Citizen Premion. He was guillotined at noon today!"

An awful silence fell upon the clamorous multitude, and some among them remembered the mysterious warning which had been uttered at the Red Inn, and the words of Père Michel. All eyes were fixed upon a tall figure, wrapped in a cloak.

"You are mad!" cried the more courageous. "Whoever you may be, you are dreaming. Premion is no traitor, but an honest republican. He was here but lately, and expected to return."

"True!" said the stranger, "he left the Red Inn of Saint Lyphar, taking the train for Nantes. On his arrival, he was arrested there on the accusation of one who had acted as his spy. The charge was grave, that of being in correspondence with the *émigrés* at Coblentz. His treasonable papers were given up by his accuser!"

Again there was a pause, and then a fierce shout of "Down with Premion! Down with the traitor, who would have sold the people!"

"Aye, down with Premion and all his works," said the stranger, "and I warn you now to desist from this task which Premion commanded. Leave the chateau to the proper authorities."

Such a cry of rage broke out at these words that it scared the sea-birds in their nests on the Marais and woke the echoes of the Bocage—a furious outburst of cries, yells, denunciations, blasphemies. The tiger, deprived of its prey, is not more ferocious; the cobra, uncoiled from its expected victim, is not more venomous. They would tear the castle stone from stone. They would burn it to ashes, once pillaged of its treasures. It was a wild scene, terrific even, with the background of an angry sky, dull red on ashen gray. The passions of those fierce men rose tumultuous as a tempest and turned against the stranger, who stood calmly with folded arms looking at them. He had risked much on that one venture, and he now knew that, with all his marvelous ingenuity and resourcefulness, he, Jambe d'Argent, was powerless to save the chateau, or even his own life. He very deliberately drew his sword, as a ring of brutal-faced ruffians began to close about him.

"He is an aristocrat!" they shrieked. "He seeks to save this nest of aristocrats and deprive honest republicans of their due. We shall burn the chateau, and roast him at the same fire which consumes it."

"Meantime, I should advise you not to draw too near," observed Jambe d'Argent; "this is a very keen blade of mine, a pretty piece of steel, with a pretty taste in *sans-culottes*."

"Tear him to pieces! Close upon him! Break his sword into bits!" screamed the furious Jacobins, waving their red caps.

But it was those in the background who did most of the screaming, and the men who were quite close to Jambe d'Argent were in no haste to draw near. Something in the resolute mien of the man awed them, and the flash of his sword seemed to dazzle their eyes. Yet not even the strongest will nor the most determined bravery on the part of one man can long prevail against a horde of lawless men, whose passions are inflamed by greed or cruelty. A simultaneous yell was uttered, and a mad rush from behind thrust forward those surrounding Jambe d'Argent, so that his sword was all but ineffectual. Pikes were raised above his head, muskets pointed at his heart, and one gigantic ruffian brandished a flail close to the head that had planned so many a daring scheme for faith and royalty. Jambe d'Argent looked about him an instant, commending his soul to God, and raising his eyes to the angry heavens. But another sound broke upon the stillness:

"*Vive la religion Catholique!* Long live the King! Soldiers of the Catholic and Royal Army, upon them!"

It was the voice of Gaston de la Roche André, and his gallant young figure presently leaped into the very center of the throng, his sprig of oak in his hat and his scapular in his buttonhole. Close following him came Richard, with a whole host of others, wearing the well-known uniform of La Vendée.

"Men of Saint Lyphar!" cried Gaston, "save first our leader, and then the chateau!"

A scene of wild confusion ensued.

"We are betrayed! The brigands are upon us!" cried the republicans; "the brigands of La Vendée!"

And they strove to fly, to hide themselves, the few who thought of fight turning with a dreadful desperation upon those redoubtable peasant soldiers who had inspired in the ranks of the republicans everywhere so great a dread. Cursing, swearing, howling, they struck madly about with whatever weapon came to hand, some turning in their mad terror upon their own comrades. Never had the chateau witnessed such a spectacle. Never had the village of Saint Lyphar heard such sounds.

"Count Gaston! Duplessis!" cried the Vendeans, using those names as battle-cries, "lead on, we follow! To the rescue! to the rescue!"

"Aye, to the rescue, brave hearts!" cried Gaston, snatching off his hat and waving it, as he dashed through the close circle about Jambe d'Argent, which remained rather through fear and bewilderment than from any purpose of renewing the attack upon the redoubtable leader.

"I am safe, my children," said Jambe d'Argent, smiling upon them, as Gaston and Richard almost at the same time reached his side, "but we have work to do yet. We must purge Saint Lyphar this time, or her atmosphere will become poisoned."

He was off to a distant part of the field as he spoke, his sword flashing as some magical talisman, his tall form everywhere conspicuous.

"It is the devil!" cried some of the republicans, flying before him.

"It is Jambe d'Argent, who has brought the brigands here by his accursed sorcery," cried others, slinking away out of his path.

"Give quarter!" cried Gaston, "give quarter to those who yield. Remember, we are the Catholic and Royal Army."

"But to those who resist, death!" cried the sterner Richard.

It was late when the fight was done. The republicans, dispersed, were flying in all directions, striving to leave Saint Lyphar behind them, save the score or so who had fallen and the prisoners who had been taken. That night the Red Inn of Saint Lyphar was full of sullen-faced men, securely bound and guarded. They were the revelers of the previous nights and the pillagers who robbed the Red Inn of its glory. But despite its half-ruined state, never in its history did a more joyful little party sit down to supper than upon that night. The materials for the supper were brought chiefly from the castle, and prepared and served by Henriot.

The three leaders of La Vendée, Jambe d'Argent, Count Gaston, and Duplessis, were seated with Count Robert, still weak and worn from his recent sufferings, and Dumartin, gradually recovering under the influence of food and wine. A fire glowed upon the hearth, casting its glow over the brown beams of the ceiling, the lozenged window, and the pleasant group at table. They chatted gaily of past changes, of hopeful prospects for the future, with many a tender remembrance of the dear ones beyond the water.

"All is well so far," said Jambe d'Argent. "We shall have fighting yet to do, and, if we are spared, we shall see stranger events, for our country has to shake off a fearful nightmare. But it is gradually becoming purified, and the people are awaking from their mad dream of blood. They have seen the heroism of the priests, the true priests of God, and here in La Vendée they have thrown in their lives with the people, and have led the hosts of God. Here in our Breton provinces, and, thank God, throughout France, noble and heroic deeds have almost outnumbered those of horror. Meanwhile, let us pledge the Catholic and Royal Army!"

The toast was drunk, standing and in silence.

"Jambe d'Argent!"* cried Gaston, raising his glass once more, "our inspired leader, who has so often saved us."

"The family of Roche André!" cried Richard next.

"Our brave Duplessis!" added Gaston, while at suggestion of Count Robert, a final toast was drunk:

"To Dumartin and the RED INN OF SAINT LYPHAR."

<hr />

*A brave soldier and leader in the Vendean army was known by this quaint title of Silver Leg, because of a band of silver which he wore to conceal a wound. But I have not followed the historical narrative in his regard, either as to station or particular achievements. I have borrowed merely his name. The same is the case with Duplessis. All the other characters are fictitious.

OTHER TITLES AVAILABLE FROM ST. AIDAN PRESS

View a sample chapter from each title at www.staidanpress.com.

THE QUEEN'S TRAGEDY
by Msgr. Robert Hugh Benson

"Upon the publication of former books of mine several kindly critics remarked that the reign of Mary Tudor told a very different story with regard to the Catholic character. It is that story which I am now attempting to set forth as honestly as I can."

$19.00 — 364 pages. Available at amazon.com.

THE NET
by Agnes Blundell

"Roger felt a freezing dew break out upon his forehead. The net was over him it seemed; in vain he told himself that he could establish his identity. His head was worth forty pounds to the vile creatures at the stair foot, and once in their clutches who knew if he could ever communicate with his friends?"

$16.00 — 264 pages. Available at staidanpress.com.

REDROBES
by Fr. Neil Boyton, S.J.

Thirteen-year-old orphan Jacques gets into trouble in Quebec, and decides to run away to Huronia and become an interpreter for his Jesuit guardian, Father John Brebeuf. But his journey along the Iroquois-infested river may not be so easy as he hopes!

$17.00 — 300 pages. Available at amazon.com.

THE ANCHORHOLD
by Enid Dinnis

Editha de Beauville had wealth, wit, and beauty; yet a chaplain's sermon drove her to give up the world and enter the religious life. But could a proud, strong-willed noblewoman embrace the poverty and self-abnegation, and particularly her full seclusion in an anchorhold? Read on to learn how she fared, and how her life affected those around her, including Sir Aleric, her erstwhile suitor, now a crusader knight; Fr. Nicholas, a young priest who was quite bright, and thought so; and Fiddlemee, the witty yet wise court jester whose past held a surprising secret.

$14.00 — 194 pages. Available at amazon.com.

THE SHEPHERD OF WEEPINGWOLD
by Enid Dinnis

Sir Robert Luffkyn has purchased the manor of Weepingwold from the noble but impoverished de Lessels, intending to make the renamed Luffkynwold a busy center of his tanning trade. He sends Petronilla, last de Lessels, to the nuns, and plucks little Brother Kit from the cloister to become the new parson of the long-abandoned church. How will Father Kit fare with the parish and his own soul? Will Petronilla find her true vocation? And is there really a witch in the parish?

$14.00 — 202 pages. Available at amazon.com.

SCOUTING FOR SECRET SERVICE
by Fr. Bernard F. J. Dooley

Frank and George are going to spend their summer vacation in the Adirondacks, thanks to Frank's uncle Ed. But once they get there, they realize something fishy is going on. Can they trust Pete, their Indian guide, or is he mixed up in it too? And is Frank's mysterious uncle really behind it all?

$14.00 — 188 pages. Available at amazon.com.

THE MASTERFUL MONK
by Fr. Owen Francis Dudley

Brother Anselm comes back to England to counter the Atheist's efforts to destroy the influence of Catholic morals. Between his lectures he is drawn into a struggle for the soul of Beauty Dethier, who is Catholic but fascinated by the "freedom" of the world and the Atheist. It will take more than argument to save her from disaster.

$18.00 — 342 pages. Available at amazon.com.

WILL MEN BE LIKE GODS? & THE SHADOW ON THE EARTH
by Fr. Owen Francis Dudley

Father Dudley's first two books on human happiness are published together here—his rare collection of essays together with a novel which illustrates the essays and introduces his most famous character, the Masterful Monk.

$15.00 — 216 pages. Available at amazon.com

CANDLELIGHT ATTIC & ODD JOB'S
by Cecily Hallack

"I am continually hearing stories—exquisite ones—which would be proof enough to any soul that God is an Infinitely Understanding Person. But usually for the very reason of their nature, they are private—keepsakes between the soul and God."

$14.00 — 192 pages. Available at amazon.com.

THE HAPPINESS OF FATHER HAPPÉ
by Cecily Hallack

Shingle Bay did not know what to make of Fr. Savinius Happé. He was a cheerful, rotund Franciscan, a famous author of books on everything from Etruscan civilization to Alpine meadows to beetles, and someone who had never quite mastered the English language. His jovial demeanor concealed a wisdom that alternately bewildered, astonished, but ultimately won over the people of Shingle Bay.

$10.00 — 112 pages. Available at amazon.com.

CON OF MISTY MOUNTAIN
by Mary T. Waggaman

"It had been a long night for Con. Just what had happened to him he was at first too dazed to know. Dennis had flung him into the smoking-room with no very gentle hand, turned the key and left him to himself. And, sinking down dully upon a rug that felt very soft and warm after the hard flight over the mountain, Con was glad to rest his bruised, aching limbs, his dizzy head, without any thought of what was to come upon him next."

$14.00 — 190 pages. Available at amazon.com.

NON-FICTION

THE STORY OF THE WAR IN LA VENDÉE AND THE LITTLE CHOUANNERIE
by George J. Hill, M.A.

The brave French Catholics of the Vendée and neighboring provinces rose up in arms when the revolutionary government replaced their priests with clergy who had renounced the Pope. Though they lacked money, allies, and were divided by disputes, they did not cease to fight until they had secured the open practice of their Faith. Here is the story of their devotion and courage against the advocates of liberty, equality, fraternity, and death.

$18.00 — 342 pages. Available at amazon.com.

CATHOLICISM AND SCOTLAND
by Compton Mackenzie

Much has been written about the desperate fight that English Catholics waged to keep the Faith, but Scotland's Catholic history is little known. Have you ever heard of David Beaton, Cardinal Archbishop of St. Andrews, and his struggles? Or of Fr. Ninian Winzet, who boldly challenged Calvinist champion John Knox to a public debate? Read this book and find out about the Scots who sought to defend their country and their Faith from the onslaught of Protestantism.

$12.00 — 138 pages. Available at amazon.com.

DOMINICAN SAINTS
by the Novices of the Dominican House of Studies

Here are related the astonishing lives of fourteen saints of the Dominican Order, including St. Dominic, St. Catherine of Siena, Pope St. Pius V, St. Rose of Lima, St. Vincent Ferrer, and more. An encyclical on the Dominican Order by Pope Benedict XV and a list of all the Dominican Saints and Blesseds (as of 1921) complete this wonderful introduction to the "Dogs of the Lord."

$19.00 — 392 pages. Available at amazon.com.

www.ingramcontent.com/pod-product-compliance
Lightning Source LLC
Chambersburg PA
CBHW030228180626
46810CB00008B/3027